A HUNDRED SHADOWY FIGURES

rode across the wide prairie to meet in deadly rendezvous with the most notorious outlaw in all of Texas—Veck Sosna!

Trailing the skulking figures, Slade halted briefly to scan the dark countryside. "We're getting close," he breathed. "Better ease up." Suddenly the whicker of his horse resounded alarmingly in the stillness. Now would he be discovered?

Nerves tense, Slade turned in the opposite direction. He steered toward the mouth of a near canyon when six riders appeared from within. One tall, hard-faced shadow loomed across the rest, and Slade knew then that he was trapped—by Sosna—in a deadly crossfire. That this was the grim rendezvous—on the
TRAIL OF BLOOD AND BONES.

TRAIL OF BLOOD AND BONES

Bradford Scott

WILDSIDE PRESS

ONE

RANGER WALT SLADE, NAMED BY THE PEONES of the Rio Grande River villages, *El Halcón*—The Hawk—rode to Brownsville, Texas, from the south. After zig-zagging across the Mexican States of Chihuahua, Coahuila, Nuevo Leon, and Tamaulipas. Quite a roundabout route, but necessary, under the circumstances.

"Shadow, once again the hellion did the unexpected," he murmured to his tall black horse. "I was just about sure for certain that when he skalleyhooted out of Texas, he'd head for the mountain country of Sinaloa. That's just what he didn't do. Instead, he headed east, raising hell and shoving a chunk under a corner, as usual. Left his customary trail of blood and bones in his wake. Took time out to rob a bank, a couple of stage coaches and a railroad express car, and the devil alone knows what else. At least six killings to his credit that we're sure of. Has got all northern Mexico in an uproar.

"Oh, it's Veck Sosna on the loose again, all right. No doubt in my mind as to that. Everything ties in with the Sosna method. And he's already managed to collect a following of side-winders. Six in the bunch that robbed the Coyame bank and killed the cashier. Now it looks like he might be sliding back into Texas. Well, perhaps we'll be able to learn something in Matamoros or Brownsville."

Reining the big black in, Slade hooked one long leg comfortably over the saddle horn and rolled a cigarette. He made a striking picture in the dying light, the last rays of the setting sun etching his sternly handsome profile in flame. Very tall, more than six feet, with broad shoulders that slimmed down to a sinewy waist.

His face was in keeping with his splendid form—lean, deeply bronzed; the grin quirkings at the corners of his rather wide mouth lessened somewhat the tinge of fierceness evinced by the prominent hawk nose above the powerful jaw and chin beneath. His countenance was dominated by black-lashed eyes of a very pale gray; cold and reckless

5

eyes, but in their depths little devils of laughter seemed to lurk, devils that could spring forward in warmth and kindliness on occasion, or could instantly become devils, not at all laughing, did the incident of the moment warrant such a transformation. His pushed-back "J.B." revealed crisp, thick hair so black a faint blue shadow seemed to lie upon it.

Slade wore the homely but efficient garb of the rangeland —Levi's, the bibless overalls favored by the cowhand, faded blue shirt with vivid neckerchief looped at the open throat, well scuffed half-boots of softly tanned leather.

About his lean waist were double cartridge belts, from which the carefully worked and oiled cut-out holsters carrying the black butts of heavy guns protruded.

And from the butts of those big Colt Forty-fives his muscular hands never seemed far away.

His mount was in keeping with the rest of him, full eighteen hands in height, black as a starless night, his coat a satiny gloss that caught the light, his eyes large and filled with fire and intelligence.

Slade sat smoking thoughtfully and gazing toward Matamoros, the Mexican town on the south bank of the Rio Grande, across from Brownsville.

Matamoros was really not much older than Brownsville but had been battered and battle-scarred into a semblance of antiquity. It was a typical Mexican Border town with sleepy plazas, and a ragged edge of squalid pole and adobe huts heming it in. It had been burned a couple of times and pillaged more than once.

The Plaza de Hidalgo, surrounded by better homes and buildings, was the chief center of activity. There was a huddle of curio shops, miniature bazaars and saloons. Outward from the plaza were low, one-story structures, mostly of brick, built close against the narrow sidewalks.

Matamoros always reminded Slade of an old *peon* wrapped in a tattered *serape,* sombrero pulled low, drowsing in the sun; but with a ready knife beneath the blanket.

That was Matamoros, lethargic, somnolent, but a powder keg only needing a spark to blow sky high.

Slade rode through the *Calle Abasolo,* the City Market Place, vibrant with colors, and filled with odors and sounds, where everything from food to jugs, kettles and mats were for sale. He was headed for a *posado,* or inn, that adjoined a cantina and, like the more primitive *meson,* catered to man

6

and beast. The establishments were owned and operated by one Amado Menendez, fat, jolly, but plenty salty if necessary, with whom Slade was well acquainted.

"Time for you to put on the nosebag, jughead," he told the horse. "You've been on sort of short rations for the past week. Amado will remember you and see to it that you get the best. I can use a good surrounding like Amado's puts out myself, for a change, and a decent bed to sleep in. Then we'll see what's what."

Amado's cantina was not far from the river, in a section that enjoyed a somewhat dubious reputation. Here more than one plot and counterplot had been hatched, sometimes to the detriment of Brownsville across the river, the Texas town receiving, with almost equal frequency, the bullets and the refugees of battles between rival factions in Matamoros. Deserters from the various factions looted both sides of the river with cheerful impartiality. Which tended to distrub peaceful citizens of both communities.

Near where the cantina stood, with its back windows looking across it, was a wharf to which the small river steamers tied up to unload cargo designed for Matamoros, when they paused before crossing the stream to Brownsville.

In front of the cantina was a hitch-rack at which a number of shaggy Mexican ponies were tethered. Slade dismounted and dropped the split reins to the ground.

"Be right back after you," he told Shadow, and entered the saloon, from which came the sound of music and gay voices.

Although it was early, there was already a fair crowd at the bar and the tables. Heads raised as the tall Ranger pushed his way through the doors. Amado Menendez, the owner, was at the far end of the bar. He stared, then came hurrying forward, his rubicund face wreathed in smiles.

"*Cápitan!*" he cried, "is it really you? Verily, wise is the voice of our people that says, 'Mountain never meets with mountain, but at daybreak or at even man shall meet again with man.' For now in the glow of the sunset I find El Halcón, my friend!"

He seized Slade's hand and shook it vigorously, chattering the while in both Spanish and his Mission-taught English.

"Ha! *amigo*, doubtless you hunger and thirst," he said. "We will drink and we will dine."

"First my horse," Slade replied.

"Sí the beautiful *caballo!"* Amado exclaimed. "Him I remember well. With my own hands will I lead him to his rest. Come!

"Ha! he remembers me!" he added delightedly, as Shadow pricked his ears forward and blew softly through his nose.

With his arm across the horse's neck, he led the way past the inn, which shouldered the cantina, and to the building which adjoined it on the far side and housed the stable. The old keeper in charge bobbed and grinned, and bowed reverently to Slade.

Shadow remembered him, too, and permitted himself to be led to a stall where all his wants would be provided for. Slade picked up his saddle pouches and his rifle.

"The best room in the *posado,*" said Amado. "There we will place them, where *Cápitan* will woo slumber this night."

The room in question proved to be large, airy and comfortably furnished, boasting two wide windows.

"And now to attend to the wants of the inner man," said Amado. "Here is the key to your room. Fortunately I have been very busy since I arrived at the cantina, after a long and busy night last night and have not yet breakfasted; so I too will do full justice to the repast. Come!"

As they sat down at a table near the dance-floor, Slade glanced through the windows on the far side of the room and saw a small, blunt-nosed river steamer poking her bow toward the wharf.

"The Bravo, she makes the run from Brownsville to Laredo and back," said Amado. "She's coming down from Laredo now. Will tie up here till morning, then unload some stuff and cross the river to Brownsville. Often does that. Gives her crew a chance for a night on the town here in Matamoros. Skipper prefers for them to have their bust here, I've a notion. Quieter than Brownsville, as a rule."

"Her crew Mexicans?" Amado shook his head.

"I think he may have one or two Mexicans," he replied. "Most of his deckhands are old deepwater men who are getting along in years, some of them stove up from accidents. The sort that can't take the rough seas any longer and sign up with the little Gulf coastwise trading vessels. Some drift up to Brownsville from Port Isabel or even over from Corpus Cristi and go to work on the river steamers. I think some of them live in Matamoros—married Mexican girls. The Bravo carries a rather large crew for her size, for

8

she has a lot of loading and unloading to do at wayside stops. Sort of a river tramp."

"What does she pack?" Slade asked.

"Oh, most everything, especially on the up-river trip," Amado replied. "A lot of hides and tallow coming down, and sometimes a good deal of wool. Quite a few sheep ranches between here and Laredo and it's cheaper for them to ship by boat."

Formerly, Slade knew, river traffic out of Brownsville had been heavy. Now, however, it was confined to a relatively few small steamers that picked up cargo wherever they could.

Amado glanced around and lowered his voice. "Sometimes those little boats carry a pretty valuable lading," he remarked. "Gold shipments from the mines, or money being transferred from one bank to another. Usually, however, nothing of any consequence."

Slade nodded and eyed the approaching vessel with interest.

The dinner arrived, and it was a good one, to which Slade and his host both did full justice.

"That is better," said Amado, with a sigh, as he poured ruby wine into goblets. "One must hunger to really appreciate good food." He glanced down at his ample waistline.

"Me, I always hunger," he chuckled. "And it takes much to tighten such a belt as clasps my middle."

"So here's to tighter belts," Slade said, and raised his glass.

"That toast I will drink with the, how you say it, gusto," replied Amado, clinking rims.

"And now, *Cápitan*," he added, "would it please you to tell me why you have visited Matamoros? There must be a reason."

Slade told him, in detail. Amado listened attentively without interruption. He shook his head when Slade paused.

"Such a *hombre* as you describe has not entered my place, of that I am sure," he said. "But there are other cantinas beside *La Luz*, my establishment. In one of those he may have been noted. I will make inquiries, and without delay. A moment, please."

He arose and crossed to the end of the bar, where a tall, slender young man with a dark and savage countenance, and glittering black eyes stood. Aside from his height, he

9

looked more Yaqui Indian than Spanish. Amado engaged him in low-voiced conversation. The other nodded and, a moment after Amado returned to the table, he sauntered out.

"If there is aught to learn, Estevan will learn it," Amado said to Slade. "A wild young man. Wild and fierce, but a rooted rock beside one in time of trouble."

"He looks it," Slade agreed. "Yaqui?"

"His mother's mother was the daughter of a Yaqui chief, his grandfather and his father Spanish. Well, amigo, I must leave you for a while; I have much to do and it looks like a busy night. Rest, and drink deep. Truly it is a day when El Halcón is my guest. El Halcón, the friend of the lowly, the champion of all who sorrow, who are oppressed and who know wrong. I am honored."

"Thank you," Slade replied. "I too am honored, to be the guest of one who is upright and honorable."

Amado beamed happily and ambled off.

TWO

LEFT TO HIS OWN DEVICES, Slade relaxed comfortably with a cup of coffee and a cigarette, and gave himself over to thought. He wondered if his hunch that somewhere in the neighborhood of Brownsville he would contact Veck Sosna was a straight one. It was indeed based on sound reasoning. With all northern Mexico seething because of his depredations and the *rurales*, the very efficient Mexican mounted police, storming on his trail, it seemed logical that he would slide across the river into Texas till things cooled down a bit.

And there were plenty of pickings in the country surrounding Brownsville. To the north and west were big and prosperous cattle ranches. And there were stage lines, and the transcontinental railroad not far off. Also the narrow-gauge road that had been built from Brownsville to Port Isabel.

All of which spelled opportunity to a shrewd and enterprising bandit leader; and Veck Sosna was both.

He wondered uneasily if Brownsville and its environs might not be in for a reign of lawlessness similar to that inaugurated by Juan Nepomuceno Cartinas years before. Cartinas had terrorized the section and had even raided Brownsville, and held the city captive for forty-eight hours.

Veck Sosna, he believed, was as capable as Cartinas and had the same ability to attract daring and ruthless followers.

Veck Sosna! graduate *summa cum laude* of a great university, who could write Ph.D. as well as M.D. after his name. A mad genius who had somehow taken the wrong fork of the trail. El Halcón versus Veck Sosna! A saga of the West that would be talked about for many a year to come.

Well, if Sosna had any such notions in mind it was up to him, Slade, to thwart the sadistic devil. Although the wily outlaw leader had so far always managed to elude capture, Slade had already more than once smashed his organization and sent Sosna himself high-tailing to fresh pastures.

11

"Twice I figured he was dead, and he wasn't," he told his unresponsive coffee cup. "And twice he managed to wriggle out of my loop when I felt sure it was tight around him. Oh well, the hellion's luck can't hold out forever, I hope."

With which he dismissed Sosna from his mind for the moment and concentrated on his surroundings, which were calculated to quicken the pulses of a young man who had spent most of the past month in the saddle, and with no time for diversion.

Now the bar was crowded with a colorful gathering. The card tables were occupied, a roulette wheel spun gaily, the faro bank was going strong. A good orchestra played soft music and there were a number of pretty *señoritas* on the dance-floor.

"It is *fiesta*, a feast day," remarked Amado Menendez as he paused for a moment at Slade's table. "Many people from the other side of the river join in the celebration."

Inconsequentially, Slade recalled that it was the morning after just such a celebration in Matamoros, aided and abetted by citizens from across the river, that Cartinas had swept into Brownsville where the town folk were placidly sleeping off the effects of the hilarious night's entertainment. It didn't seem likely that history would repeat itself, but Veck Sosna was more unpredictable than Cartinas had ever been.

Oh, the devil with Sosna! Slade again put the disturbing side-winder out of his mind and vowed to keep him out the rest of the night, discounting the fact that Sosna himself might have something to say about that.

As Slade was debating a whirl on the dance-floor with one of the attractive *señoritas*, Estevan, the young man Amado sent to try and gather information returned. His dark hawk face was impassive, but Slade thought the glitter of his black eyes was more pronounced.

However, he did not glance in Slade's direction, nor did he approach Amado. Instead, he found a place at the bar and ordered a drink. A few minutes later he sauntered to the dance-floor where Slade shortly saw him dancing with one of the *señoritas*, a tall, nicely formed girl with curly hair as black and glossy as a raven's wing in the sunlight. Apparently he had learned nothing. Slade directed his attention elsewhere. He ordered more coffee and had nearly finished the cup when a girl paused at his table. Glancing

12

up he saw it was the very attractive young lady with whom Estevan had danced.

"Will the *señor* dance?" she asked. Her eyes met his and he seemed to read more than was spoken in their depths.

"Why not?" he smiled, and rose to his feet. They approached the floor and Slade encircled her trim waist with a long arm. Walt Slade liked to dance, and he could dance. So could the girl. And soon he was thoroughly enjoying himself. But as they drifted gracefully through a momentarily open space she spoke, her voice little above a whisper, her lips hardly moving.

"After the number, take me to your table and order wine," she said. "It will give me the excuse to linger. I must speak with you."

Slade nodded his understanding and after the number was finished led the way to the table. Amado himself came hurrying in with a bottle of wine. He filled the glasses with a flourish, glanced meaningly at Slade and with a low bow departed. As she raised her glass, the girl laughed gaily and nodded, as if in answer to some quip; but words fluttered through her laughter.

"Estevan feels sure that the man you seek was here in Matamoros in the early afternoon. At *El Toro* on Rio Street near the river, where the rivermen drink. His friend works there, on the floor, and she remembered the man, for he was not one easy to forget. Tall, almost as tall as yourself, and broad, with eyes that seemed to burn. A handsome man, she said, but—a woman's intuition, perhaps—evil. She said there were five others with him and that they remained for some time, drinking and talking. She watched them ride out of town by way of the Camino Trail."

"Which runs west," Slade interpolated.

"That's right," the girl replied. She laughed again and raised her glass, but her eyes, which in contrast to her hair, were blue, slanted sideways toward the bar.

"Estevan thought it best not to come to you or to Amado, for in here there are often eyes that see and ears that listen, and he felt that the less heard and the less seen the better."

"He was right," Slade agreed. He shot her a searching glance.

"You are not Mexican?" She shook her head.

"No, I'm a Texan," she replied. "My father married Amado's sister. My parents died, not far apart, two years

13

ago. Amado sent me to school and when I got back to Brownsville I wanted to go to work. As you know, the day when women allow their relations to support them in idleness is fast drawing to a close. So after considerable argument, I persuaded Uncle Amado to let me work here, on the floor and helping him in various ways. I'm Dolores Malone."

"Good Lord!" he exclaimed in comical dismay. "Black Irish and Spanish, with a dash of Yaqui thrown in for good measure, I suppose. No wonder Amado allowed himself to be *persuaded;* he's a prudent man of good judgment."

She laughed merrily and Slade realized what a pretty girl she was.

"Oh, it's not so bad as all that," she protested. "I'm not such a firebrand as my name appears to indicate. Really I'm quite meek, and rather timid." El Halcón did not appear impressed.

"Do you live with Amado?" he asked. She shook her curly black head.

"No, I live in Brownsville, with Amado's younger sister, who is a widow; her husband was killed during one of the uprisings a few years back.

"I'll have to be getting back to the floor," she said, adding softly, "will I see you again?"

"You will," he replied, with an emphasis that heightened the color in her cheeks. She cast him a smile over her shoulder as she tripped back to the floor. Slade's eyes followed her with appreciation.

She had handled the situation adroitly, he thought. It was customary for her partner to buy the girl a drink after each number; she would sit the next one out with him. Just as it was a routine practice in the Matamoros cantinas for the girls to circulate among the patrons between numbers. Her pausing at his table would cause no comment.

Estevan had played his hand well, too; were there someone in the place who took an interest in the movements of El Halcón, a communication from the young Mexican would have been noted, and perhaps read aright. Slade did not believe that Veck Sosna had one of his men stationed in the cantina, but if he had learned by some chance that the man he considered his nemesis was present, it was not beyond the wily devil to do just that. Sosna was the essence of the unpredictable.

He ordered more coffee and for some time sat smoking

14

and studying the crowd, and not a man passed in or out of the swinging doors that he did not note. Finally, he came to the conclusion that if there was somebody around who took an interest in his movements, he was certainly keeping well under cover.

It was still not so very late, but Slade was tired after a long day in the saddle, with very little sleep the night before. Besides, the place was growing noiser by the minute and he felt that a little quiet wouldn't go bad.

"I think I'll call it a night," he told Amado, who paused at the table for a minute. Lowering his voice, "Thank Estevan for me, and thank you, too. You both did me a big favor. Incidentally, Dolores is a smart girl."

"And a trial to her old uncle," Amado sighed. "One word from me and she does just as she pleases. But she is nice, don't you find her? And beautiful?"

"Both," Slade agreed, heartily. Amado chuckled. "Sleep well," he said. "Tomorrow I see you."

Slade caught Dolores' eye and waved to her. Then he left the cantina and repaired to his room in the *posado*, opening the door with the key Amado provided.

It was quiet and peaceful in the room, a welcome relief from the cantina's hullabaloo. The radiance of the late moon streamed through the east window. The other window opened onto the river, which glowed silver in the wan light. Without bothering with the lamp, he drew a chair to the window and sat gazing across the stream at the lights of Brownsville on the far shore. Below was the wharf, against which the black bulk of the small steamer, the Bravo, loomed. The gangplank was lowered, but there was no sign of life aboard the vessel. Only one wan light showed, doubtless in the captain's cabin where very likely a lone deck hand or perhaps the skipper himself stood watch, while the rest of the crew celebrated in town.

The muted strains of music drifting through the cantina's back windows were soothing, its babble of voices but a drowsy hum. Slade began to really enjoy himself as he pondered the information Estevan garnered. He wondered if Sosna had doubled back on his tracks and was headed west again. However, he thought it unlikely. A few miles west of the town was a ford which could be negotiated by horses when the river was low, as it was at the moment. Quite likely the cunning outlaw preferred to slip across the river via the ford rather than by way of the bridge from Ma-

15

tamoros, where such a band would be conspicuous. Well, he'd cross to Brownsville himself tomorrow and see if he could pick up the trail.

As he gazed dreamily at the star dimpled water, his eyelids grew heavy, and he was just about ready to call it a night and go to bed when something within his range of vision snapped him wide awake again.

Stealing slowly across the wharf was a group of men, six or seven in all, it appeared. Slade watched them slow their gait even more as they neared where the Bravo was moored. They halted, seemed to gaze earnestly at the boat. Then they crept forward again, headed for the gangplank. Just who and what they were, the Ranger wondered.

Some of the crew coming back from town? Possibly. But why that stealthy approach? To all appearances they were anxious to avoid detection, especially by somebody who might be watching from the Bravo. Slade grew very much interested. He stood up, moved back from the window a little and scanned the terrain about the wharf; it was devoid of life other than the crouching group that had now reached the gangplank.

At the foot they hesitated for a moment, then went up it swiftly. On the deck were tall stacks• of hides, bundled and awaiting unloading; the group vanished in their shadow, reappeared, heading for the captain's cabin in which a light glowed.

As was usually the case with the small river steamers, the captain's cabin was a deck house. In deference to the heat, the door stood open. The group went through it with a rush.

A sound split the silence—a clatter as of an overturned chair, a gurgling cry, then silence.

16

THREE

Nerves tense, Slade peered out the window and could see nothing save that single glow of light. He whirled, left the room and sped down the stairs, across the lobby, which was untenanted, and into the street. He rounded the corner of the building, raced a few steps and the wharf was before him.

It lay silent and deserted, just as was the Bravo, to all appearances. But there was little doubt in Slade's mind but that there was life aboard the Bravo, malevolent life. Also, very likely, death.

With the greatest caution, he glided across the wharf to the foot of the gangplank. He paused, scanning the deck above, and saw nothing. A moment later and he was on the deck, his eyes fixed on the glow that seeped through the half-open door of the cabin. Keeping in the shadow of the stacked hides, he passed it, striving to reach a point from where he could peer in. He reached the edge of one of the hide stacks, and stepped from the shadow.

Just in time Slade saw the loom of the man beside the cabin door. He was going sideways toward the stack when a lance of orange flame gushed through the darkness; a bullet ripped the brim of his hat. Jerking both guns he fired, left and right. There was a choking grunt and the thud of a falling body. The cabin erupted a storm of exclamations. Slade ducked behind the stack as guns blazed in his direction. Shoving one gun around the edge of the stack, he emptied it in the direction of the cabin door. A yelp of pain and a wailing curse echoed the reports, then another bellow of gunfire. Bullets thudded into the hides but none came through. He shifted guns and fired three more shots around the edge.

A ringing voice boomed an order. There was a clatter of boots on the deck, a steady stream of shots. The outlaws were retreating to the gangplank, firing as they backed toward it. Slade crouched low. He did not dare peer around the stack, and he was saving his last three cartridges against a dire need; the hellions might take a notion to rush him.

Abruptly the firing ceased. Slade waited a tense moment, heard the clatter of boots diminishing. He risked peering around the edge of his shelter and saw shadowy figures racing across the wharf.

The cantina was a pandemonium of yells and curses. A head thrust out one of the windows, jerked back as a bullet smashed the glass above it. Slade bounded forward and emptied his gun after the vanishing figures, but with little hope of scoring a hit. He reloaded with frantic speed as he sped to the gangplank and down it. There was no sign of the outlaws, but to his ears came a clatter of hoofs fading westward. His voice rang out, piercing the turmoil in the cantina.

"Amado!" he shouted. "Amado, come here. Bring Estevan with you."

"*Sí, Cápitan!*" howled answer from the cantina. A moment later Amado came puffing around the corner, clutching a sawed-off shotgun. Beside him was Estevan, a cocked Colt in one hand, a long knife in the other.

"*Cápitan,* we come!" bawled Amado. "Where are the *ladrones?*"

"Gone," Slade replied, "but I think they left one behind. Let's go see."

Heads were peering cautiously around the corner of the stable, shouting questions.

"Let them come," Slade said. "Best for everybody to see what happened."

He led the way up the gangplank and across the deck to the cabin door. Lying beside it was the body of a man.

"Ha! one did stay behind!" exclaimed Amado. "Now he burns in *el infierno. Cápitan,* what happened?"

Slade was peering into the cabin.

"Take a look," he said.

On the floor lay another dead man who was dressed as a deckhand. The handle of a knife protruded between his shoulders.

"Sosna leaves no witnesses," Slade remarked. He gestured across the cabin.

Against the far bulkhead stood a ponderous iron safe, a new model. Sticking in the door was the slim length of a steel bit, the hand drill still attached.

"Already one hole started beside the combination knob,"

18

Slade remarked. "Fifteen more minutes and the knob would have been out, the safe opened. Looks like there must be something of value in that box." He turned to the swearing saloonkeeper.

"Amado," he said, "send somebody to try and locate the captain of this tub. Send somebody else to fetch the *alcalde*. I want him and the skipper to see things just as they are. Don't let anybody touch anything."

Amado crackled orders to the crowd that had pushed close but did not attempt to enter the cabin. Several men dashed down the gangplank and vanished in the darkness.

Slade drew up a chair that was not bolted to the deck, sat down and rolled a cigarette. Estevan hovered over him, glowering suspiciously in every direction and fingering his knife. Under the threat of his savage face and his long blade, the crowd remained at a respectful distance outside the door.

It seemed the shooting had aroused half the town, for the throng was constantly augmented by new arrivals volleying questions that nobody could answer.

"Can you tell us what happened, *Cápitan?*" Amado pleaded.

Slade told him, briefly. Amado swore in two languages, Estevan adding a few pungent Yaqui expletives for good measure.

"And if it weren't for your courage and quick thinking, the *ladrones* would have gotten away with whatever they were after," Amado declared. "One more good deed to the credit of El Halcón." Estevan nodded emphatic agreement.

"Here comes the *alcalde*," somebody shouted. A moment later the mayor, a portly individual with a pleasant face and sharp eyes, pushed his way into the cabin.

"*Cien mil diablos!*" he gasped, staring at the body of the sailor on the floor.

"Not a hundred thousand devils, but enough, *Don* Pedro," said Amado.

"But what is the meaning of this?" demanded the bewildered official.

Amado told him, vividly. The mayor walked over to Slade and solemnly shook hands.

"*Cápitan*, I am honored," he said. "*Gracias* for what you did. What is in the safe? I know not for sure, but I feel safe in saying there is a large sum of money from a Laredo bank. I was informed that they intended to dispatch it to Browns-

19

ville by steamer, because of the rash of stage and train robberies with which we have been plagued of late. The plan was supposed to have been a guarded secret."

Slade nodded, not at all surprised; Veck Sosna always seemed able to learn everything. If El Halcón had been inclined to be superstitious, he would have believed the hellion put into practice some gift of divination or mental telepathy.

"When the *Señor* Clark, the steamer's captain, arrives, doubtless he can tell us for sure," added the mayor.

At that moment the *jefe politico*, the chief of police, put in a tardy appearance. The mayor glowered at him.

"And you, I suppose, were swilling *pulque* in some *pulqueria* while murder and robbery were being done," he accused his subordinate. The policeman looked abashed and muttered something of just pausing to quench his thirst with a glass of the Mexican beer.

"Besides, I knew not there was aught of value aboard the boat," he added defensively. "Why should one keep watch over hides and tallow?"

The mayor grunted and did not appear mollified. But before he could frame a scathing retort, an elderly man with grizzled hair and a weather-beaten face entered. He swore bitterly as his eyes rested on the slain seaman. Slade gathered that he was the Bravo's captain, which proved to be the case.

The skipper swore again when what had happened was outlined for him. He turned to Slade, held out his hand.

"Thanks, cowboy, for sorta evening up the score," he said. "And the Company will want to thank you too, and a mite more. Better'n twenty-five thousand dollars in that box. Yes, you did a fine chore and I won't forget it." He gestured to the dead sailor.

"That poor swab was with me for five years," he added. "Most of my boys have been sticking around for quite a spell. I've got so I sorta look on them as if they were my own kids; hurts when something happens to one of them."

"I can well understand," Slade remarked. "Captain, who all knew the money was to be sent down the river on the Bravo?"

"Why, only the bank officials and myself were supposed to know," the skipper replied.

"Could some of your seamen have learned of it?" Slade asked. The captain hesitated.

20

"Well, some of them might have guessed it, at least guessed we were carrying something of value," he admitted. "The cashier of the bank delivered the money to me in person and watched me lock it up."

Typical of the way "official secrets" were guarded, Slade reflected. However, he merely nodded and let the subject drop. Sosna had somehow learned the money was on the steamer. How? Perhaps he'd find the answer to that one later.

"And now," suggested the mayor, "suppose we drag that dead *ladrone* in here where it's light and examine him."

The body was hauled in unceremoniously by the heels. The dead man appeared to be an ordinary individual of medium height and build. His pockets disclosed nothing of significance, so far as Slade could see.

"Anybody recognize him?" he asked. There was a general shaking of heads. Which was what El Halcón expected. He raised one of the fellow's hands and scrutinized it, then the other; he turned to the Bravo's captain, who was squatting beside him.

"What do you think?" he said.

"The same as you do," the skipper replied. "Yep, he was a deepwater man not so long back; only hauling on lines will put that sort of marks on a swab's hands. Nothing strange about that, though; we get quite a few of 'em in Brownsville. Mostly Gulf men who sign on with the little coastwise trade wind ships. A lot of 'em have been around quite a bit. Sort of settle down here."

"I suppose some of your hands are former deepwater men?" Slade suggested.

"About half of them, I reckon," the skipper admitted.

"And this fellow would have been able to speak their language and associate with them without attracting any attention."

The skipper shot him a shrewd glance. "Uh-huh, I reckon," he replied. "Wouldn't be surprised if he could use his ears good, too."

"Exactly," Slade nodded.

Another example of how Veck Sosna worked, and of his uncanny ability to corral followers who would best serve his purpose. The man in question mingled with the Bravo seamen and listened to what was said. Perhaps was able to adroitly steer the conversation into a discussion as to what cargo she bore coming down from Laredo. Some loquacious

21

individual might have mentioned the bank cashier's visit with the captain, the significance of which Sosna would have interpreted correctly. Yes, the Sosna touch.

His deduction was corroborated a moment later when the Bravo seamen, having heard what happened, came streaming aboard. They mingled their curses with the skipper's and grouped around the dead outlaw.

"Say, I remember this lubber!" one exclaimed. "He was drinking with us in Laredo. Got to gabbing about ships he'd sailed on. One of them was the Gloucester, a schooner I signed with once. He knew all about her, all right." A couple of his companions nodded agreement.

The skipper glared at them. "And I suppose some of you swabs blabbed about what you thought was in the cabin safe," he said accusingly.

An uncomfortable silence followed. Slade felt pretty sure that one or more of those present suffered twinges of conscience but preferred not to incur the captain's wrath by saying so. Well, it didn't matter one way or another who was guilty of imprudent loquacity. The damage had been done, providing Sosna with opportunity of which he had been quick to take advantage.

Slade stood up. "Well, *amigos,* I'm going to call it a night," he said. "You will hold an inquest, *Don* Pedro?"

"*Sí,* in the afternoon," the mayor replied. "This one we will give holy burial. Let the other—" he glowered at the dead outlaw—"let him go unshriven and unannealed, his soul dragged hell-wards weighted by his sins. Sleep well, *Cápitan,* I will attend to all."

Accompanied by Amado and Estevan, Slade made his way through the crowd of curious gathered on the wharf.

"*Vive* El Halcón!" a voice cried. The cheer was given with a will. Slade smiled and raised his hat. "Thank you, *amigos,*" he called answer.

"A glass of wine before you retire?" Amado suggested.

"I'll settle for a cup of coffee," Slade replied. "Wouldn't go bad right now."

"*Bueno!*" said the cantina owner. "Dolores will joy to see you are all right. She was in tears when we left in answer to your call."

When they entered the cantina and sat down at a vacant table—most of the patrons were grouped at the bar, discussing the recent happenings—Dolores joined them.

"I was terribly frightened when I heard that awful shoot-

22

ing," she told Slade. "I just knew you were mixed up in it. And when you called Uncle Amado your voice sounded as if you were hurt."

"I wasn't," he replied cheerfully. "Just a mite excited, I guess."

Dolores shrugged her slim shoulders disdainfully. "I don't think you ever get excited, or show any emotion of any kind."

"You may learn different," Slade warned, his eyes dancing.

For some reason known best to herself, the remark caused her to blush and lower her lashes.

"You look terribly tired," she said, solicitously. "You should go to bed without delay."

"That's a notion," he agreed. "I am tired and I'm going to do just that; it's been a busy night. See you tomorrow."

"I'll be here in the late afternoon," she replied. "*Hasta luego!*"

"*Hasta luego*—till we meet again."

FOUR

SLADE DID GO TO BED, AFTER CLEANING AND OILING HIS GUNS, and was asleep almost before his head hit the pillow. He awakened shortly after noon, greatly refreshed and fit for anything. After breakfast at Amado's *La Luz*, he and the cantina owner attended the inquest.

It was more formal and stately than the rangeland type across the river, but the verdict was similarly terse and to the point. Slade was commended for the part he played. The deckhand met his death at the hands of parties unknown whom the authorities were urged to apprehend and bring to justice. The slain outlaw was now tasting of the flames of *infierno*, it was hoped.

Afterward, everybody reparied to Amado's cantina for a drink. Slade and the owner occupied a table in a corner near the dance floor, where they could talk without interruption.

"And you feel sure that the outrage was planned and executed by the man Sosna you seek?" said Amado.

"No doubt in my mind," Slade replied. "I didn't get a look at him, but I heard his voice, a voice I'll never forget. Yes, it was Sosna, all right; the chore was typical of him."

"And were it not for your courage and intuition, it would have succeeded," Amado commented.

"Luck played a considerable part," Slade replied. "I just happened to sit down by the window at just the right time and spotted the hellions sliding up the gangplank."

"And tackled them all, singlehanded," Amado observed dryly.

"And I slipped a bit there," Slade added. "I was careless and neglected to be on the watch for a lookout posted by the cabin door, and very nearly got my comeuppance in consequence. Well, I guess you can't think of everything."

"Nobody has been able to so far, I would judge," Amado agreed. "and you believe the *ladrones* crossed the river to Texas?"

24

"That's my opinion," Slade conceded. "By way of the ford to the west of Matamoros, I'd say."

"And you intend to pursue him?"

"I do," Slade stated. "That is," he added grimly, "if it doesn't turn out he's pursuing me, which has been the case more than once in the past."

Amado chuckled. "Sounds like the carrousel, the—merry-go-round," he said.

"It goes around, all right, but there's not much merry about it," Slade smiled.

El Halcón versus Veck Sosna! The ablest and most fearless of the Texas Rangers pitted against the most cunning, most ruthless outlaw Texas ever spawned!

Slade pushed his empty coffee cup aside and stood up. "I'm going to take a little ride," he announced. "Tell Dolores I'll see her later."

"I'll do that," Amado promised. "She will await you eagerly."

When Slade reached the stable, Shadow whinneyed joyfully. The old keeper bowed and smiled.

"He likes not to be inactive," he observed, apropos the tall black.

"I'll give him a chance to stretch his legs a mite," Slade said as he cinched the saddle into place. "We'll be back."

"*Adios, Cápitan,*" said the keeper. "*Vaya usted con Dios* —go you with God."

Leaving Matamoros and Brownsville behind, Slade rode west on the Camino Trail, which ran close to the river's edge. After a while the flat lands on the far side of the stream gave place to low rises thickly grown with brush, continuing to the ford and beyond.

At the ford, Slade reined in and gazed across to the heavy chaparral growth that ran close to the water's edge.

The ford was a narrow ridge beneath the water, something like the Indian Crossing at Laredo, which is a ledge of limestone rock lying just below the surface of the water, and in dry seasons becomes exposed. Here there was never any exposure and the water was deeper. And, similar to the Indian Crossing, below the ford the river swirled and eddied, flashing and glittering and spuming rainbowed arcs of spray.

Such peculiar geological phenomena interested Walt Slade. He knew that this eastern section was on the fringe of the earthquake belt, the manifestations of which were often disturbing to the west coast. Such formations as the

25

ones just mentioned evidenced subsidence or elevation not far in the past, geologically speaking, and it was with the eye of a geologist that he studied and understood them.

Shortly before the death of his father, subsequent to financial reverses which entailed the loss of the elder Slade's ranch, young Walt had graduated from a famous college of engineering. He had planned to take a post-grad course in special subjects to round out his education and better fit him for the profession he had determined to make his life work. .

However, at that time it became economically impossible and he was sort of at loose ends and trying to make up his mind as to just which course of action to pursue. So when Captain Jim McNelty, his father's friend, the famous Commander of the Border Battalion of the Texas Rangers, who recognized good Ranger material when he saw it, suggested that he come into the Rangers for a while and pursue his studies in spare time, Slade decided the idea was a good one. Long since he had gotten more from private study than he could have hoped for from the post-grad and was eminently fitted for the profession of engineering. .

However, in the meanwhile Ranger work had gotten a strong hold on him, which doubtless canny Captain Jim figured would be the case, and he was loath to sever connections with the illustrious body of law enforcement officers. Engineering could come later, he was young; he'd stick with the Rangers for a while longer.

Which explained his professional interest in such terrestrial manifestations as the Indian Crossing and the ford on which he gazed.

"Well, horse, here goes," he said. "Maybe we can pick up a trail over there that will lead us to something. Not much travel on the north bank and half a dozen gents riding fast should have left some marks of their passing."

Shadow didn't argue the point and sloshed along in water that rose almost to his barrel.

As they neared the middle of the stream, where the water in the channel below the ford was very deep, Slade constantly studied the approaching north bank.

It was El Halcón's inherent watchfulness and meticulous attention to details, plus his keen eyesight, that saved him from the drygulcher's bullet. He saw the gleam of reflected sunlight as the hellion shifted his rifle the merest trifle before pulling trigger, and was already going sideways and

26

down in the saddle, almost to the water, when the slug yelled through the space his body had occupied the instant before.

But Slade knew he was a setting quail in the full blaze of the sunlight and outlined against the water. To try and shoot it out with the rifleman holed up in the brush would be tantamount to suicide. There was but one thing to do, a devil of a chance to take, but he had no choice. He whirled Shadow downstream. His voice rang out, "Take it!"

Shadow took it, with a squeal of protest. Straight into the swirling, eddying waters below the ford he plunged, casting up a cloud of spray, going clear under. Slade slipped from the saddle and went under with him.

Up they came, blowing and gasping, and as they broke surface, bullets smacked the water beside them; but the drygulcher could see little to shoot at and none of the slugs found a mark. Then the current seized them and hurled them downstream toward a bend a few hundred yards distant.

But as he battled with all his strength to reach the nearer north shore, Slade began to fear that he had just traded a quick death from lead poisoning for a somewhat slower one by drowning. For here the ever unpredictable Rio Grande ran like a millrace and the water in the channel was deep and cold. For half the distance to the bend he did not gain a yard. Weighted by his guns and his clothes, he could barely keep his head above water, and Shadow was having trouble, too. Slade gripped the bridle iron with one hand and paddled furiously with the other. His arms were growing heavy as lead, there was a band as of hot steel about his chest, tightening, tightening, shutting off his laboring breath. His heart was pounding, red flashes stormed before his eyes.

He went under again, broke surface gasping and retching; looked like it was curtains.

They reached the bend and with a surge of renewed hope, Slade realized that they were in an eddy that was whirling them toward the north shore. A moment later Shadow's irons clashed on stones. He gave a prodigious snort and surged forward, Slade clinging to the bridle iron. Another instant and his boots scraped on the bottom and he was reeling and stumbling through the shoaling water. Together they struggled ashore, Shadow to stand gulping and gurgling, Slade prone on the warm sands.

Gradually his strength returned. He regurgitated some of the water he had swallowed and felt better. Sitting up, he hauled off his hat, which had been kept in place by the chin strap, and batted it free of water. Removing his boots, he emptied them and managed to struggle back into them. Then he stood up, shook himself and wrung out his clothes as best he could. Fortunately the sun was hot and he was already beginning to steam.

All the while he was keeping a sharp watch upstream, against the chance the drygulcher might put in an appearance around the bend. He made sure his Winchester was free in the boot—it would take no harm from the wetting.

"Into the edge of the brush, horse," he said. "We'll hole up there for a while; don't want to get caught settin' again."

Physically he was feeling pretty good; but mentally he was thoroughly disgusted with himself and in a very bad temper. Outsmarted again! Sosna had figured what his move would be and had set a trap for him; and he had blithely blundered into it.

"And nothing but plain bull luck saved us," he growled to Shadow, overlooking the part his own acute perceptions had played. He smiled wryly as he recalled his remark to Amado Menendez, that in this deadly game of hide-and-go-seek it was sometimes difficult to be sure just who was the pursued and who the pursuer. Sure worked out that way this time. Still watching the brush-flanked bend in the trail, he drew forth his waterproof pouch of tobacco and matches and rolled and lighted a cigarette.

"Guess we can take a chance on a brain tablet," he told Shadow. "Won't make enough smoke to be seen and the wind's blowing from the west, so the hellion can't smell it. Seems ridiculous to think he could even with the wind blowing the other way, but if Sosna himself happens to be somewhere around, I wouldn't put it past him. Now I wonder what he figures I figure to do? The answer to that one could be mighty important."

He smoked the cigarette down to a short butt, which he pinched out carefully and cast aside. For several more minutes he stood gazing toward the bend in the trail; it showed no signs of life.

"Horse," he said, "we're going to play a hunch. It's evident that the hellion isn't riding down this way to try and learn what happened to us. I've a notion he'll figure that if we weren't drowned, we'll continue to wherever we were headed for when we tackled the ford. Which would mean that we'd ride west on this trail. Perhaps he hightailed when we went into the drink, but then again perhaps he didn't. He could still be holed up waiting for another chance. Sosna doesn't take kindly to failure, and the fellow may be reluctant to go and report that for all he knew he did fail. The whole business seems to be sheer nonsense, his arriving at such a conclusion; just doesn't make sense. But then nothing the Sosna bunch does seems to make sense. Let's go!"

Mounting, he rode diagonally up the brush clad slope. Shadow didn't like it but registered his disapproval in a single disgusted snort, then forged ahead, avoiding as many thorns as possible.

Slade smiled grimly as he reflected that now, at least, the outlaws were on Texas soil and under his jurisdiction as a Ranger. In Mexico his only authority had been what he packed on his hip, and there was always the chance that he might find himself in exceedingly hot water. This was much better.

Finally he reached the crest of the rise where the growth was even heavier than farther down the slope. Shadow wriggled and wormed his way through the chaparral strands until they arrived at a point Slade believed was not far from being directly above where the drygulcher had been holed up and possibly still was. As far as he dared go on horseback. He slipped from the saddle, dropped the split reins to the ground and gave Shadow a pat.

"Take it easy, now," he whispered. "Can't take a chance any longer on the racket you make shoving through the brush. Be seeing you."

Silently as the shadow of the great mountain hawk for which he was named, he drifted down the slope, pausing often to peer and listen. He followed a slantwise course for a while, until he was sure he must be directly above the point from which the drygulcher's bullets had come. Now it should be less than a hundred feet down the sag. That is, if the fellow hadn't moved. He might have slipped farther down the slope, but Slade doubted it. Farther up he would have a better view of the trail where it curved around the growth, following the bend of the river. Slade slowed his pace to a crawl, careful to snap no twig, to step on no dry branch, to move no stone.

The sun was close to the western horizon now and it was

already gloomy under the thick growth. The hush of evening had descended, broken only by the sleepy chirps of birds. Slade strained his eyes to pierce the deepening shadows, and he began to believe that his thorny ride and stalk had been for nothing; there was naught to be seen, nothing to be heard. Looked very much like the killer had hightailed. Instinctively he quickened his gait a little.

Then abruptly he halted to stand rigid. From nearby had come a sound, faint and musical, the jingle of a bit iron as a horse tossed its head. The devil was still there!

But blast it! where was "there?" Must be close, unpleasantly close. Had he been spotted creeping down the slope? Was the muzzle of a gun swinging in his direction, eyes glinting along the sights? A nice thought! He stood tense and motionless, his glance probing the shadows ahead,

bleday, N.Y., 1948.

drew a breath of relief as nothing happened. He risked another forward step, and saw the drygulcher.

He was lounging against the trunk of a small tree, less than half a dozen paces distant, his eyes fixed on the trail below. Slade's pulses leaped exultantly; he had the hellion "settin'!" Take him alive and perhaps force him to talk. He drew his right-hand gun, glided forward another step. His lips opening as if to speak, he sensed rather than saw movement to his right. There were two of the devils!

Sideways and down he went. A gun blazed and the slug whipped through the crown of his hat. He fired at the flash, rolled over and over. The drygulcher by the tree whirled with a yell of alarm. Bullets stormed from two directions, kicking up spurts of dust, fanning his face with their deadly breath. He shot as fast as he could pull trigger, left and right, left and right!

A gurlging scream knifed through the uproar, the thud of a falling body and a wild thrashing about. Slade whirled over on his side, saw the second killer looming huge and distorted in the gloom, almost over him. He fired point-blank, tried to surge erect. Something crashed against his skull and the world exploded in flame and roaring sound, and a cyclone-rush of blackness.

30

FIVE

WHEN SLADE RECOVERED CONSCIOUSNESS, he realized that
he could not have been out for long. The sky was reddening
with sunset and there was still some light under the growth.
The brush was shrouded in utter silence. Where were the
two killers? He tensed, his right hand mechanically gripping the gun he still held. The silence remained unbroken.
He raised his left hand to his throbbing head and discovered a sizeable lump just above his left temple. What in
the jumping blue blazes had happened?

Dazedly, he summoned enough strength to sit up, and
recoiled, swinging his gun muzzzle to bear on a huddled
form by his side.

Quickly, however, he realized there was nothing to fear;
it was a corpse that lay motionless beside him. He glared
about in search of the second drygulcher, barely made out
what was left of him under the tree against which he had
leaned. What *had* happened?

He groped about, found his second gun. Automatically
he ejected the spent shells from the Colts and replaced them
with fresh cartridges. Laboriously he got to his feet. His
head ached abominably, but his mind was clearing. Glancing down, he saw that the hand of the dead man beside him
was clamped over the butt of a six-shooter. He stared at
the iron, and reconstructed what had happened.

"Of all the freakish things!" he exclaimed aloud. "As the
hellion fell, almost on top of me, he lashed out with his gun
barrel and connected with my head, darned solidly. Well,
thank Pete he didn't pull the trigger at the same time or I'd
likely have more than a lump to show for it."

Yes, a bit freakish, but admitting of a quite simple explanation. Just the muscular reflex of a man shot through
the heart, jerking forward the hand gripping the gun. In
fact, the only thing really freakish about the incident was
that his head should have been in such a perfect position to
get larruped.

31

With the aid of matches, he examined the bodies. Both were hard-case looking hellions with nothing outstanding about them. The man by the tree had gotten one through the throat. Their pockets discovered nothing he considered significant. Just the usual trinkets packed by range riders, plus considerable money. He struck another match and by its light regarded the unsavory pair. From complexion and facial contours, he judged that each had a fair dash of Indian blood, very like Comanche, which was interesting. He straightened up and glanced around.

After some searching he located the pair's horses, tethered to a tree trunk. They were good looking animals in the best of condition. He examined the brands closely and quickly arrived at the conclusion that they were Panhandle country burns. Which also was interesting.

Leaving the animals as they were for the moment, he returned to the dead outlaws, struck more matches and studied their stark countenances. He straightened up, stared at a star that was winking through a rift in the growth.

"Well," he told the twinkler, "it looks like *Senōr* Sosna has managed to get word to some of his Comacheros up in the Panhandle and they've ambled down this way to join him. Wonder how many more of the devils are with him or on the way. This is beginning to look darn serious."

If his surmise was correct, the situation had indeed developed a disturbing angle. Veck Sosna had been the leader of the sprawling outlaw band, the Comancheros, which had terrorized the Canadian River Valley and Oklahoma Border country before Sosna, fleeing the relentless pursuit of El Halcón, had made his way south to the Big Bend region and Mexico.

Snake-blooded, utterly ruthless, they had apparently inherited all the vices and none of the virtues of two races, combining the driving force of the White with the callous cunning of the Red, for all or nearly all could boast Comanche blood in varying degree. If Sosna had managed to gather some of them about him, there might well be some lively times in store for the Border country around Brownsville.

Slade debated what to do about the bodies, finally determined to leave them where they were. He'd notify the sheriff of Cameron County, with whom he was acquainted, and let him dispose of them as he saw fit.

Returning to the horses he untied them, removed the

rigs, and left them to fend for themselves until the sheriff or somebody picked them up. They'd make their way down to the grassland and do okay.

With a final glance around, he groped his way through the darkness to where he had left Shadow, who greeted him with a disgusted snort.

"Okay, okay," he said. "We're getting out of here pronto, and we're steering shy of that blasted ford, too; no sense in bucking it in the dark. We'll head for Brownsville and cross the bridge to Matamoros; that'll be a mite easier going, at least."

Shadow didn't argue the point and nosed his way down to the trail, where Slade sent him east at a fast clip.

Everything considered, despite the problem that confronted him, El Halcón was in a fairly complacent frame of mind. Things had worked out a lot better than he'd hoped for a couple of times, and he felt he'd taken the trick this time. *Señor* Sosna would be in a very bad temper when he realized that his little scheme to rid himself of his enemy had backfired. Would give him a good deal of a jar, and Slade believed the episode might well work to his advantage inasmuch as that when Sosna thoroughly lost his temper he also lost some of his caution, and was inclined to take reckless chances. Well, he'd see.

Although he did not think he had anything to worry about at the moment, Slade rode warily; Sosna was utterly unpredictable. He felt relieved when he sighted the lights of Brownsville. Familiar with the town, he headed for the sheriff's office and had the luck to find that official relaxing comfortably in a chair, his boots on his desk, picking his teeth after his evening meal.

The boots hit the floor with a bang when Slade entered. The sheriff, a bulky old veteran of the Border turmoil, leaped to his feet and held out his hand.

"Well! well!" he boomed. "How's the notorious outlaw today?"

Due to his habit of working under cover as much as possible and often not revealing his Ranger connections, Walt Slade had built up a peculiar dual reputation. Those who knew the truth declared him to be not only the most fearless but the shrewdest of the illustrious band of law enforcement officers. Those who did not were wont to vow that he was just another blasted owlhoot too smart to get caught, so far, but who would get his comeuppance sooner or later.

The deception Slade practiced worried Captain Jim Mc-Nelty, who feared that his Lieutenant and ace man might come to harm at the hands of some trigger-happy deputy or marshal or some gun slinger out to get a reputation by downing El Halcón, and not past shooting in the back to achieve his ends. Captain Jim growled, but Slade only laughed and minimized the danger, at the same time pointing out that with the owlhoot fraternity thinking him one of their brand, avenues of information were open that would be closed to a known Ranger.

"Fine as frog-hair," he replied to Sheriff Calder's facetious greeting.

"Take a load off your feet," invited the sheriff, casting him a searching glance. "Say, you look as if you'd been swimming with your clothes on. And how'd you get that goose egg on the side of your head?"

Slade sat down, rolled a cigarette and told him, in detail. Calder did not interrupt, save by muttered profanity as the tale progressed.

"Two of 'em laid out in the brush, eh?" he commented, when Slade paused. "Okay, we'll pack 'em in tomorrow if you'll show me where they are. Maybe the coyotes will beat us to them, though, and get pizened. But who in blazes is this blasted Sosna you're telling me about?"

"The shrewdest, meanest and all around orneriest outlaw Texas ever produced," Slade replied. "I first contacted him in the Canadian River Valley country, up in the Panhandle, where he'd been operating for quite a while. Local authorities appeared powerless against him, so Captain Jim sent me to look things over."

"Which should have been the finish of Sosna," the sheriff grunted.

"But it wasn't," Slade admitted. "So far as I was concerned, it was just the beginning. I did manage to get him on the run. Followed him into the Cap Rock hills and by way of the Trail of Tears to the hidden valley where the Comanches used to take their women and children captives. With the help of some poor devils he held as slaves there, I was able to clean out his bunch; but Sosna escaped. I trained him from the hills to the open prairie and thought I had him in my loop, but just at the wrong moment a darned freight train came along. Sosna tied onto it and got away.

34

Then he dropped out of sight for a while, but not for long."

Slade paused in his narrative to roll another cigarette. The sheriff waited expectantly.

"Finally I got a line on him," the Ranger resumed. "He was down in the lower Big Bend country and Mexico, raising heck and shoving a chunk under a corner as usual. Don't need to go into all the details, but again I managed to get rid of his bunch, but again Sosna got in the clear. I chased him from his hangout in Mexico to the Rio Grande at Boquillas. The river was in flood, no horse could swim it, and I thought I had him. But there is an overhead conveyor system there that ferries ore from the mines across to the Texas side of the river by way of a cable stretched across the stream. Sosna left his horse, went up the conveyor tower like a squirrel and hand over hand along the cable."

"And made it to the other shore?" the sheriff interpolated. Slade shook his head.

"I went after him via the cable. Hanging onto it over the middle of the river we shot it out. I got him in the arm. He fell and the water washed him into Boquillas Canyon. Everybody insisted that no man could live through that canyon with the river in flood, but sometimes I think Sosna is a devil instead of a man. He did live through the canyon. I wasn't particularly surprised to learn, nearly a year later, that he was alive and kicking and going strong down toward the Border east of the Big Bend. Always original, he'd cooked up a new scheme. He was preying on emigrant trains from east Texas and Louisiana and having a field day for himself."

"And you lit out after him again?"

"Naturally," Slade replied. "Once more I finally got him on the run. That time I was sure he was done for. Closing in on him, I saw him try to jump a sheer-walled canyon at least sixty feet deep. His horse didn't quite make it and down they went. Looking down the wall I could see, in the clear moonlight, the bodies of man and horse lying motionless on the rocks sixty feet below. Right there I slipped a mite. I should have made sure for certain that he was dead; he wasn't. I suppose the horse landed on its feet when it struck the bottom of the canyon. Very likely the shock broke its neck; but Sosna, evidently, was only stunned. I felt sure he was really dead that time. I wasn't in very good shape myself, so instead of trying to descend into the canyon and investigate, I rode off."

"And he wasn't dead, eh?"

"Far from it," Slade answered. "You could have knocked me over with a feather when, months later, Captain Jim learned he was set up in business again, around El Paso."

Slade ceased speaking for a moment to roll and light another cigarette.

"So, to make a long story short, as the saying goes, I headed for the El Paso country, got a line on the hellion and once again did stop most, if not all, of the bunch he'd gotten together. He and I met face to face and shot it out. I was never sure whether I nicked him—he was holding a corpse in front of him as a shield, a hellion I'd gotten dead center a second before. But he sure nicked me. I caught one in the leg that knocked me for a loop. Sosna hightailed and the last I saw of him he was rounding a bend half a mile distant and, to all appearances, headed for Mexico. As I told you, I figured he'd head for the mountains of lower Sonora or Sinaloa; he didn't. He managed to get another bunch together while I was trying to pick up his trail and started raising the devil down in *mañana* land. I tracked him clear across Mexico but never could quite catch up with him. The nearest I came to it, as I said, was the other night in Matamoros. Now it appears he's in Texas again and squatting in your bailiwick."

The sheriff groaned dismally. "As if I didn't have enough trouble," he lamented. "Plenty of owlhoots in the brush country already, and it's beginning to look very much as if another revolution against old *El Presidente* is brewing the other side of the river. If it does really cut loose, Matamoros will blow sky high and Brownsville will, as usual, catch all the falling pieces."

"Wouldn't put it past Sosna to start one of his own," Slade chuckled.

Immediately, however, he was grave; the thought was disturbing. Would be like the canny devil to do just that, if it happened to occur to him. And with his genius for organization he'd soon have a following of fanatics ready to do his bidding without question. Slade abruptly experienced an unpleasant premonition. Sometimes there is meaning in a jest, based perhaps on a subconscious evaluation of conditions. Anyhow, he wished he hadn't allowed such a notion, seemingly absurd but not necessarily so, to infiltrate his thought processes.

"And now what?" asked Calder.

36

Slade stood up. "I have a room in Matamoros," he replied. "I'm going over and clean up a bit and have something to eat. See you tomorrow."

The sheriff eyed him disapprovingly. "I like you, Walt, and I respect your ability," he said, "but blast it! trouble just nacherly follows you around. Wherever you coil your twine the devil cuts loose pronto."

"I didn't herd Sosna up here," Slade protested.

"I'm not so sure," the sheriff growled. "I've a notion that if he learned you were on his trail he hunted cover in a hurry, and the brush country to the north of here provides fine cover. Oh well, at least things aren't dull when you're around. Be seeing you."

Chuckling, Slade left the office. He reached the Gateway Bridge by way of Fourteenth Street and rode across to Matamoros. Later there would be a toll gate in the middle of the bridge and inspection booths, but at present there were not. After putting up his horse he repaired to his room for a general clean-up and a change of clothes he had in his saddle pouches.

Next stop was *La Luz*, Amado Menendez's cantina. Amado spotted him the moment he entered and came hurrying forward to greet him.

"You've had us all worried," he said. "Dolores is in the back room working on my books, a task I despise. Come quickly and allay her fears."

He ushered Slade into the back room and closed the door behind him. Dolores was seated at a table that was littered with books and papers. She sprang up with a glad cry as he approached.

"I was afraid something terrible had happened to you," she exclaimed.

"Nothing for you to worry your pretty head about," he replied. Cupping his hands about her slender waist, he lifted her lightly from the floor and kissed her. For a moment her lips clung to his. Then as he dropped her on her feet, blushing and shy, she hid her face against his shirt front. He rumpled her curly black hair and she looked up, smiling. Abruptly her big eyes widened.

"Oh, that awful bruise on your forehead! How—"

"I ran into something," he evaded blithely. Dolores regarded him doubtfully but did not press for an explanation.

"Doesn't it hurt?" she asked. He shook his head.

37

"Not a bit; I'd forgotten all about it. Had your dinner yet?"

"Not yet," she answered, "I was just thinking of eating. Have you eaten?"

"Not since breakfast," he admitted.

"Good heavens, you must be starved! Just a minute."

She riffled the papers together, closed the books. "I'm ready, come on," she said. "We'll eat together."

She opened the door and led the way to an isolated table at the corner of the dance-floor. A waiter hurried forward, smiling and bowing, to take their order.

"Wine while we're waiting?" she asked.

"I'll take coffee, if you don't mind," he replied.

"Me, too," she said. "I prefer it to wine, of which I don't drink much."

"To which your complexion attests," he said. She smiled and blushed.

They had a very jolly dinner together, for both were very hungry, and consumed it with the appetite of youth and perfect health.

"And now tell me what you've been doing, if you don't mind," she said, as the waiter refilled their coffee cups.

Slade hesitated a moment, then decided it was best to tell her everything. Sooner or later she'd get a garbled version of it, certainly after the inquest which would be held on the two dead outlaws. Her expressive eyes widened with horror as he related the incidents of the afternoon.

"Only by the mercy of God were you not killed," she breathed. He nodded sober agreement.

"But as it was, everything ended up okay," he said. "So we won't pay it any more mind."

"I can't dismiss it so lightly," she said with a sigh. "I suppose they tried to kill you because of what you did on the ship last night, yes?"

Slade nodded and did not commit himself further. He deftly changed the subject.

"Guess I'll be moving over to Brownsville tomorrow," he said. Dolores glanced at him through her lashes.

"Do you—have a place to stay in Brownsville?" she asked. He shook his head.

She seemed to hesitate a moment. "My aunt has a room she rents, it's vacant now," she said softly.

"That will be just fine!" he replied, with a heartiness that brought color to her cheeks. Again she seemed to hesitate.

"Any reason why you can't move in tonight?" she asked. "If not, I'll leave early and we can cross the bridge together and get home before my aunt goes to bed."

"Better and better!" he exclaimed. "We'll do just that."

"We'll try and make you feel at home," she said demurely. "Now I must get back to work. You'll wait here for me?"

"I will," he promised.

She smiled at him. "That makes me feel better," she said. "I don't see how you can manage to get into trouble here. I'll tell Uncle Amado that Aunt Teresa is going to take you under her wing; he reposes great confidence in Teresa."

"And in his niece?"

She made a face at him and hurried to the back room, pausing a moment to speak with Amado at the far end of the bar.

A few minutes later Amado strolled over to the table and occupied the chair Dolores had vacated.

"And now, *amigo,* you will be in good hands," he said. "They are both capable women and will look after you. By the way, on the alley back of the house is a stable where you can find quarters for your horse; an *amigo* of mine owns it. Dolores keeps her *caballo* there."

"She rides?"

"To and from work every night, and long rides across the rangeland. She loves the wind and the sun and the open road. A fit companion when you ride for pleasure, as all who are born to the rangeland do at times."

"I am fortunate in finding such companionship," Slade replied.

"Even the wild hawk of the mountains must come to rest at times," Amado said gently. "You ride a lonely trail, *amigo.*"

"There are recompenses."

"Aye! for one who sows the seeds of good along the way. El Halcón has many friends who love him."

"I am indeed fortunate," Slade repeated, and meant it.

"Good fortune comes to those who deserve it," Amado remarked sententiously. "Well, I'll have to be moving around; looks like another busy night."

SIX

THE PLACE WAS FILLING UP. Slade noticed that there were a number of Texas cowhands present. Matamoros had always been a favorite rendezvous for the cattlemen from across the river. Always there had been the friendliest of relations between the two towns. Even the war between the United States and Mexico had engendered sadness rather than bitterness and hard feelings. Both communities had been plagued by the abortive uprisings and bandit raids, deplored by the great majority of reputable citizens.

As Slade sat smoking and drinking coffee, what was to be expected occurred. Surprising that it hadn't happened before. The orchestra leader sauntered across the room, holding the guitar. He paused at Slade's table, bowing and smiling.

"Will not El Halcón sing?" he requested. "As he sang for us once before? It will be the honor and the great pleasure. Please, Cápitan."

Seeing no reason why he should refuse, Slade rose to his feet, accepted the guitar and followed the proudly strutting leader to the raised platform that accommodated the orchestra. A hush followed and all eyes were fixed on his tall figure. The leader's voice rang out, "Attention, please. El Halcón will sing." He evidently thought the announcement was all that was necessary and repeated it in Spanish.

"Can he really sing?" a young cowhand asked of his neighbor, an old-timer.

"Can he sing?" snorted the oldster. "You just wait! The singingest man in the whole Southwest they call him."

"And with the fastest gunhand," somebody else remarked.

"Gosh!" exclaimed the young puncher.

Making sure the instrument was properly tuned, Slade played a soft prelude with a master's touch. Then he flung back his black head and sang, a ballad of the range.

It was just a simple little song, the kind of a song men sing to nervous cattle on stormy nights, or around lonely campfires, but as the great golden voice filled the room with melody, cards were forgotten, the dancers paused, drinks remained untasted on the bar. Dolores Malone stood in the open doorway of the back room, her red lips parted, her eyes fixed on the singer's face.

The music ceased, with a crash of chords and Slade stood smiling at the storm of applause and cries for another.

So he sang them another, one of his own composition:

"Weary wind that walks the world
Down the night's lone corridors. . . ."

Another storm of applause. Then, in conclusion, a hauntingly beautiful love song of old *Méjico*. He handed the guitar to its owner, bowed and smiled, and returned to his table.

At the bar, a voice observed, "Some folks say he's an owlhoot."

"And some folks say the moon's made of green cheese, but I ain't never seen anybody cut a slice!" snorted the old-timer. Heads nodded sober agreement.

Dolores came over to Slade's table. "You were wonderful," she complimented him, "we all enjoyed it greatly. Now, if you don't mind, I'll go upstairs and change and then be ready to leave."

"Why change?" he asked, glancing with approval at her abbreviated dancing costume.

"As you may have noticed, this skirt is rather short and rather tight," she replied. "I fear that on horseback it would climb considerably."

"Wonderful!" he exclaimed. "Don't change!"

"Neither the time nor the place," she retorted with a laughing glance over her shoulder as she headed for the back room and the stairs that led to the second floor of the inn next door.

She was down in short order. Levi's, small riding boots and a soft shirt, open at the throat, had replaced slippers and spangled skirt. Slade again nodded approvingly.

"Not bad, either," he said, looking at the menacing gun swung at her hip. She interpreted his glance and laughed.

"I can shoot," she said, "and the ride across the bridge is rather lonely at night."

"Good company for a lonely ride," he said, nodding toward the gun. "All set? Let's go." They waved goodnight to Amado and left the cantina.

41

At the stable he quickly got the rigs on Shadow and her sturdy little pinto, and led them outside. He cupped his hands about her slender waist and easily lifted her to the saddle.

"You handle me as if I were a child!" she exclaimed breathlessly as she settled her feet in the stirrups.

"Well, you're not very big," he said, as he forked Shadow.

"I'm almost as tall as Uncle Amado," she retorted.

"But slightly less in other measurements, I would say," he commented. Dolores shot him a disdainful glance and refused to be drawn into such a controversy.

They rode slowly across the bridge, their horses' irons drumming loud on the floor boards, and continued to Jackson Street. Before a small white house, Dolores slowed the pace.

"Right around the corner is the stable," she said. "I see Aunt Teresa is still up; there's a light in the kitchen. She won't be expecting me home so early."

"Nor with company," Slade predicted.

"Oh, don't worry about Teresa, nothing upsets her," Dolores assured him.

"Accustomed to you bringing men home in the middle of the night?"

Another disdainful glance and another refusal to be drawn into a discussion.

A smiling Mexican met them at the stable door. Slade liked his looks and recalled that Amado had recommended him. So he was properly introduced to Shadow and Slade had no doubt but that the big black would be properly cared for. He shouldered his saddle pouches and they walked around the corner to the little white house.

Aunt Teresa, Amado's much younger sister, proved to be but a few years older than Dolores herself. She was small, with dark hair and laughing dark eyes, and spoke English even better than did her brother.

"Oh, don't let it bother you," she replied to Slade's apology for his unexpected appearance. "She's always dragging something home, a lost dog, a stray cat, a sparrow with a broken wing. I'm expecting horned toads and wind spiders any day now. At least a man is something original. And it's about time!"

"Teresa, you're impossible!" Dolores gasped, glancing at Slade and blushing furiously. Teresa's laughter rang like little silver bells.

42

"Well, it is," she declared. "All right, show him to his room and let him stow his pouches. The one right across the hall from yours."

"That's the only one!" Dolores said, in as near a sputter as a musical feminine voice could achieve. "You're impossible!"

"It was occupied by a nice old gentleman of near eighty," Teresa explained to Slade. "Yes he was close to eighty, so— oh, well, the world moves. I sleep at the far end of the hall, so his snoring didn't bother *me*."

"He wasn't anywhere near eighty, and he didn't snore!" Dolores snapped.

"No?" Teresa's voice was innocent.

Dolores turned to the stairs. "Come on, Walt," she said energetically.

Chuckling, Slade picked up his pouches and followed her up the stairs.

"Yes, she's impossible!" she repeated for the second time as she opened the door and lit a bracket lamp.

"I think she's wonderful," Slade disagreed. Dolores sniffed.

"Come down for coffee when you're—ready," Teresa called. "No hurry."

"Yes, she's perfectly wonderful," Slade repeated, as he gazed around the tidy and comfortably furnished room. "And cooperative," he added enigmatically, glancing across the hall at a half open door.

"What chance have I got!" Dolores lamented.

"Do you want one?" She lowered her lashes.

"No."

After they finished the coffee, Teresa gave him a searching look.

"I think," she observed, "that where you belong is in bed. You look as if you've had a hard day, and it's long past midnight."

"I did have," he admitted, "and I think I'll follow your advice."

"Go right ahead," she replied. "Sleep as late as you wish. I'll wheedle everything I want to know about you out of Dolores before I let her go."

Dolores' red lips started to frame the word, "impossible," but she desisted and bade him goodnight, her voice very soft and low. Teresa smiled, a little wistfully. Perhaps she was thinking of her own "goodnights" before Death reached out a hand.

43

SEVEN

WHEN SLADE AWOKE, SUNLIGHT WAS STREAMING THROUGH
the window. Aside from a slight stiffness and the purpling
bruise on his forehead, he felt little the worse for his
harrowing experience of the day before. For a while he lay
pondering recent happenings. Then he remembered that he
had an appointment with Sheriff Calder. He washed and
dressed and descended to the living room, where he found
Dolores. A moment later Teresa entered with a cup of
steaming coffee.

"Heard you moving about," she said. "Here, no man is
fit to live with before he's had his morning coffee. You'll
find out, Dolores. Darling! what a pretty color you have
today. Your cheeks are like roses. Don't you think so,
Walt? Reminds me of myself after—oh, never mind. Now
I'll make breakfast for us; we waited to eat with you."

She whisked back to the kitchen. Slade crinkled his eyes
at Dolores, whose cheeks grew even rosier.

After breakfast, Slade at once repaired to the courthouse
between Madison and Monroe Streets and found Sheriff Tom
Calder in his office conversing with two of his deputies.

"We're all set to go if you are," Calder said, after per-
forming the introductions. "Got a couple of pack mules for
the bodies. We'll drop a loop on our horses; see you've got
yours outside."

Half an hour later they headed west. The sheriff and the
deputies talked and joked, but Slade was mostly silent, his
black brows drawing together until the concentration furrow was deep between them, a sure sign El Halcón was doing some hard thinking.

As they drew near the bend in the trail, east of where
the two drygulchers had holed up the day before, he suddenly
called a halt.

"Tom," he said, "perhaps I'm just being foolish and over-
cautious, but I've a feeling we have no business sashaying
around the bend and up the slope. I know it sounds silly, but

44

I know the hellion we're up against and how he works. He has the darndest genius for figuring out moves before they are made."

The sheriff and the deputies looked startled. "You mean there might be somebody holed up waiting for us to show?" the former asked incredulously.

"I mean there possibly could be," Slade replied. "As I said, I know what we're up against and there's no telling what Veck Sosna will do or won't do. So why take chances?"

The sheriff tugged his mustache and swore. "What do you figure to do?" he said.

"Diagonal up the sag from here, as I did yesterday, leave the horses and the mules on the crest and slide down the slope on foot until we reach where I left the bodies," Slade explained. "Means a little bad riding and a little loss of time, but it may pay off big."

Calder shook his head dubiously as he eyed the thorny growth. He glanced toward the silent bend, shook it again.

"Blast it! you've got me worried," he complained querulously. "Sometimes I wish I'd never laid eyes on you. Didn't I say trouble just follows you around? Oh, well, have it your way. You *could* be right. Come on, boys, we'll look like a passel of green hides before we're finished with that infernal chaparral."

"Better than having our hides looking like water-eaten leaves," said Jim Bowles, one of the deputies, who appeared decidedly impressed by Slade's warning. Hartsook, the other deputy, nodded emphatic agreement.

"Let's go," said the sheriff.

Slade took a straighter course up the slope than he had previously, for he knew the mules and the horses of his companions would make much more noise than had Shadow. When they reached the crest he again called a halt.

"We'll leave the critters here," he said.

Except Shadow, the animals were securely tied. Then Slade led the way along the crest until his instinct for distance and direction told him that they were directly above where the bodies should be.

"Now comes the ticklish part," he said in low tones. "Straight down the sag, and for Pete's sake don't make a noise. If they are there and hear us coming we'll get a reception we don't like."

Very slowly and with the greatest caution, the posse crept down the slope, worming their way through the growth.

45

They were something more than a hundred yards from their goal when Slade halted abruptly and held up his hand.

"They're there, all right," he breathed. "I smell tobacco smoke."

The others sniffed, but could smell nothing, although the wind was blowing toward them from the south. But El Halcón knew his keen sense of smell had not deceived him.

"Let's go," he whispered, and resumed the slow crawl through the brush. His pulses leaped exultantly. With luck they should bag whoever was waiting down there, waiting to kill. Maybe even Sosna himself.

And then it happened, another example of the Sosna luck. Slade didn't know it, but Deputy Jim Bowles, bringing up the rear, had drawn his gun and was carrying it at full cock. He stepped on a loose stone that rolled under his foot, floundered off balance and clutched frantically at a branch to save himself from falling. The branch broke, down he went, and pulled the trigger as he fell.

The report rang out like a thunderclap in the stillness. From below came a yelp of alarm, then a volley of shots. Bullets whipped through the leaves above the posse.

"They're there!" howled the sheriff. "Come on, boys!"

They were there, all right, but they didn't stay there. Slade read aright the sudden crashing in the brush. He was not at all surprised, a moment later, to hear a still louder crashing and the thud of fast hoofs fading into the distance.

"Take it easy," he told his companions, slowing his pace. "They've given us the slip. No catching them without horses, and we can't get horses in time."

Sheriff Calder was raving profanity. "The blankety-blank-blanks!" he bawled. "Aiming to drygulch a flock of peace officers!"

"To Veck Sosna and his bunch, a peace officer is just another jigger with the forked end down and a hat on top," Slade said grimly. "Let's see what we can find down there."

They found the two bodies, the rigs Slade had removed from the horses the night before, and a couple of rifles; doubtless those used by the dead drygulchers. The horses were nowhere in sight.

"They'd make their way down to the grassland, be moseying around somewhere there," Slade said. He studied the ground near the bodies.

"Five or six of the devils here, I'd say," he remarked. "Here's a mark on a tree branch where one of them rested

46

his rifle barrel preparatory to a shot when we showed around the bend. They meant business, all right."

Sheriff Calder swore again, and mopped his suddenly perspiring face.

"And if it hadn't been for you and your knack for figuring things out, right now we'd all be lying with our toes up," he said in a strained voice. "Did you really just play a hunch that the hellions would be here waiting for us?"

"Not exactly," Slade admitted. "This feud between Sosna and myself had been going on for quite a while. I've learned a good deal about how he thinks and operates. The unpleasant corollary is that *he* has learned a good deal about how I think and my methods. Yesterday was a good example. After what happened in Matamoros the other night, he figured just what I would quite likely do—try to pick up his trail on this side of the river. So he laid a trap for me. I got careless and blundered across the ford in broad daylight, just as he reasoned I would do, and it was mostly luck that I didn't take the big jump."

"Luck?" snorted the sheriff. "Go on."

"So when he realized that the attempt of his two side-winders to kill me had backfired, he did some more hard thinking and arrived at a correct conclusion. Perhaps one of his men was in Brownsville last night and saw me ride up to your office. Anyhow, Sosna figured that today we'd come to pack the bodies to town with us. So he set another trap."

"And this time you were a jump ahead of him," commented Calder.

"In a way," Slade conceded. "I figured out what he would be likely to do and governed my actions accordingly. Something in the nature of a hunch, after all, but it paid off."

Calder glanced around. The deputies had moved off to examine the bodies.

"Think he's tumbled to the fact that you're a Ranger?" he asked in low tones.

"Frankly, I'm beginning to wonder," Slade admitted. "Not that it would make much difference to him, in my opinion. His ego is colossal, and he'd have no more regard for the Rangers than for anybody else. In his opinion, Veck Sosna is sufficient unto himself and top dog of the heap.

"And sometimes, I can't help but think that maybe he's right," he added, with a wry smile.

47

"My money's on El Halcón," the sheriff said cheerfully. "Well, now what?"

"Send the boys up for the horses and mules," Slade replied. He turned to face up the slope, gave a long clear whistle. A moment later there was a crashing in the brush and very quickly Shadow bulged into view snorting inquiringly.

"Okay, feller, we'll soon be ready to travel," Slade said, stroking his glossy neck. "Nosebag soon."

"Darn cayuse has more sense than most people," grunted Calder. "I'd be willing to bet he'd have balked at rounding that bend down there."

"I wouldn't put it past him," Slade conceded. "I recollect that when we were crossing the ford yesterday he was acting up a mite. I'd be better off to pay more attention to him."

The deputies made their way up the slope and soon returned, riding their horses and leading the sheriff's mount and the mules. The bodies, the rigs and the two rifles were loaded. First the sheriff went through their pockets, uncovering nothing but a few trinkets. A few more were scattered on the ground.

"Ghouls," Slade remarked. "They cleaned them of the *dinero* they had on them. Quite a few dollars, too."

"They'd swipe their grandmother's false teeth," growled Calder. "Anyhow, they left their hardware. Good guns; I'll keep 'em for souvenirs, unless you want them." Slade smilingly shook his head.

"I don't like ivory handles," he replied. "Too slippery. Hang them over your desk to start a collection."

"And here's hoping it builds up fast," said Calder. "All set? Let's go; I'm hungry."

With the burdened mules progress was slow, and the rose and saffron of the sunset was fading to steel gray when they reached town. The bodies were placed in the sheriff's office and as the word got around, a number of citizens dropped in to view them and compliment Slade on a good chore.

However, nobody could recall seeing either before, which did not surprise El Halcón. He was pretty well convinced that most, if not all of Sosna's present followers were the villainous Comancheros from the Panhandle and Oklahoma Border country.

Which gave the Ranger no little concern. He had a premonition that the outlaw leader was embarked on a more than usually ambitious program of some sort. One that might

48

have all kinds of disturbing ramifications. The Border country was a fertile field for the evilly ambitious and ruthless.

Juan Nepomuceno Cartinas, the Red Robber of the Rio Grande, was an outstanding example. To Texas peace officers he was a bandit and a cow thief. To many of the Mexican *peones* and landholders he was a liberator and a daring champion of their legal rights. He sacked and burned ranches of non-Latin Texans, ran off their cattle, held up stage coaches, raided towns and vanished into the brush. He attacked Rio Grande steamboats, invaded Texas territory again and again, after circling the forces of law and order that sought him, and played tag with soldiers and the Rangers. Finally the Rangers, with the cooperation of the Mexican authorities, chased him away from the Border. He withdrew into the interior of Mexico and eventually became governor of the Mexican State of Tamaulipas. A colorful achievement for a one-time Border outlaw.

Walt Slade believed that Veck Sosna was capable of just such a performance, given anything like an equal opportunity. And, which Cartinas did not have, he had a streak of sadistic cruelty in his make-up and was capable of atrocities such as Cartinas would not have dreamed.

Sheriff Calder was an intelligent and observant man. He had believed Slade when he said that Sosna had no regard for the Rangers or any other peace officer. But the sheriff also believed that he did have a healthy respect for El Halcón, and that Sosna feared him.

In the meanwhile, Slade was wondering just where Sosna would cut loose next. That he would do so and in short order, he had not the slightest doubt. Sosna would feel that in the recent episodes he had suffered defeat and would be hot to even the score, directly or indirectly. And at the same time restore the confidence of his followers, which at the moment might well be a bit shaken. A successful and lucrative raid of some sort would put them in fine fettle again. A bandit leader must keep his men busy and supplied with money if he hopes to retain their loyalty.

If he could just get a line on what the devil had in mind, and forestall it! Otherwise, somebody would be very apt to die. He racked his brains for a solution of the problem, without success. Perhaps Sheriff Calder or Amado Menendez might have a suggestion; he'd keep that in mind.

The sheriff shooed out the remaining curious. "If I don't

eat I'll topple over," he declared. "Come on, fellers, and let's surround something. Never mind those two snakes on the floor; they'll stay put."

After locking the office he led the way to a bar and restaurant on Jefferson Street near Fourteenth.

"Remember this place, don't you, Walt?" he said. "The Estero. Why it's named that I don't know, but it is. Anyhow, it's a good place to eat. Likker ain't over-bad, either. Games are straight and the girls are—nice. So I guess we could do worse."

They located a vacant table and gave their order. When the food arrived it was up to expectations, and all did full justice to it.

"That helped," said the sheriff, pushing back his empty plate with a sigh of satisfaction. "Walt, you seem sorta serious of late. Different from the happy-go-lucky young hellion you used to be."

"That was before I got into the ruckus with Veck Sosna," Slade replied. "If I ever get him off my neck maybe I will be again. That side-winder has put gray hairs in my head."

The sheriff scrutinized his black thatch. "Reckon my eyesight is failing," he observed. "I don't see no silver threads among the gold."

"I dyed them this morning," Slade alibied.

"Somebody sure dyed that lump on your forehead a nice color," chuckled Deputy Bowles. "It looks real purty."

"You should have seen it before the swelling went down a mite," Slade told him.

"Well, said the sheriff, "I think I'll have a snort to hold my chuck down and then back to the office; work to do. How about you boys? Have a drink, Walt?"

"I think I'll settle for another cup of coffee," Slade decided.

Calder and the deputies downed their snorts and trooped out. Slade remained at the table, sipping his coffee and smoking.

His thoughts dwelt on Veck Sosna. He wondered how large an outfit Sosna had managed to get together. There had been at least a half dozen men holed up in the brush and watching the trail that afternoon. He doubted if Sosna had been one of their number or that the whole of his bunch had been assigned to the chore. There was no telling how many of the Comancheros he may have persuaded to ride south, perhaps to a rendezvous somewhere in the neighborhood of

Brownsville, which appeared to be his destination as he raided across northern Mexico.

From what Slade had been able to learn, the depredations committed in the course of the ride from Sonora east had been by not more than six or seven men, but Sosna undoubtedly had more than that number on tap. Well, anyhow, he was three short, which helped some. Slade emptied his cup and left the saloon.

Outside, he hesitated a moment, then headed for the little white house on Jackson Street. Letting himself in with the key Dolores had given him, he entered the living room.

"Hello?" Teresa called from the kitchen. "Sit down and make yourself comfortable. I've got coffee and cake all ready for you."

"I've just eaten," he protested.

"You can eat again," she replied cheerfully. "Men are always hungry."

She bustled in a few minutes later, her eyes laughing.

"Dolores went to work," she announced. "She waited as long as she could, hoping you'd show up."

"I think I'll go over and ride back with her," he said, sampling the cake she set before him and deciding there was room for it.

"That's nice," said Teresa. "She'll be glad to see you, and to have company on the ride home. And to have—oh, never mind. I'll be asleep when you come in, anyhow."

"We'll try not to awaken you," Slade promised. Teresa's beautiful eyes danced.

"I'm a very sound sleeper—when I should be," she said, and vanished into the kitchen.

EIGHT

GETTING THE RIG ON SHADOW, HE RODE SLOWLY ACROSS THE bridge. His decision had been based not only on a desire to accompany Dolores on the trip back to Brownsville; he had a feeling he might hear something of interest in *La Luz*. There was not much going on in the section that Amado Menendez and his associates didn't know about. Also, the cantina got a cosmopolitan crowd; news from both sides of the river filtered through *La Luz*.

It wasn't very late and Matamoros was still lively. He stabled his horse and repaired to the cantina, which he found crowded.

To Slade, sensitive to impressions, it seemed that the place was pervaded by an air of suppressed excitement amounting almost to apprehension. Men grouped together talking in low tones, evidently discussing something of vital interest. He noted that at times these groups shot glances at other groups, drew closer together and lowered voices still more.

Dolores waved to him from the dance-floor. Amado sauntered over to greet him as he found a place at the bar. He asked a conventional question or two as regards to his health and activities, speaking so that all nearby could hear. But through his chatter slid a low-voiced mutter, "Sit at a table where we can talk."

Slade nodded the merest trifle. Amado raised his voice, "Be seeing you—chores to do." He ambled back to the far end of the bar and engaged his head bartender in conversation.

Slade took his time over his drink, replying to nods and greetings from various quarters. Placing his empty glass on the bar, he made his way to a vacant table near the corner of the dance-floor.

"Coffee," he told a smiling waiter.

Dolores smiled at him but did not approach the table; she was dancing with a jolly-looking young cowhand, laughing at his quips. Her color rose as she met Slade's quizzical

52

gaze and over her partner's shoulder she made a moue at him. Slade chuckled and sipped his coffee.

Some little time passed before Amado came across the room, carrying a bottle and a couple of crystal goblets. He sat down, filled the glasses ceremoniously and raised his in salute.

"What's in the wind?" Slade asked.

"Trouble," Amado replied sententiously.

"Yes?"

"Yes. There is a rumor. Whence it came no one seems to know, but it spreads like wildfire."

"What sort of a rumor?" Slade asked, although he had an uneasy presentiment as to what it was.

"A rumor of *la revolución*," Amado replied. "There is a whisper that says a *libertador* has appeared, who will raise an army, defy *El Presidente* and restore the land rights to the people on both sides of the river. It will come to nothing, of course, the time is not yet ripe, but it will mean bloodshed, rapine and looting if it really gets under way. Opportunists have before seized such a pretext to enrich themselves, leaving their misguided followers to suffer the consequences, after vanishing with their ill-gotten gains."

Slade whistled under his breath. His hunch, vague though it was, had proven to be a straight one. Sosna really had something in mind bigger than robbery and casual murder. If such a movement really gained impetus, it would drench the Border country in blood. And there was a radical difference from other uprisings which had plagued the Border.

Cartinas and others of his ilk had, to an extent at least, the interests of the people at heart. Cartinas in the beginning, for instance, had become incensed over the treatment of the *peones* by unscrupulous politicians and landholders. Whereas Veck Sosna had regard for none but himself. The sufferings of others meant nothing to him. He was for Sosna, first, last and always. And here he had found a fertile field for the advancement of his own interests. Already there was much unrest along the great river, and not altogether without cause.

The unfortunate Diaz land policies, already being put into effect, would eventually result in more than ten million persons losing prescriptive rights to hithertofore inalienable communal lands of free villages, and becoming *peones* on the *haciendas* which would absorb the erstwhile village

53

lands. The masses were alive to the danger and were frantically seeking means with which to thwart the edict. Under such conditions, Slade was certain, an eventual great socio-economic upheaval was inevitable. History was to prove him right. Meanwhile such uprisings as might be planned by Sosna would result only in turmoil and suffering.

To make matters worse, self-seeking politicians on the north side of the river had managed to get laws passed which discriminated against the Texas-Mexicans and encroached on their rights as American citizens.

So the time was ripe for serious trouble. The Cartinas episode had cost hundreds of lives, both American and Mexican, and an estimated half million dollars in monetary damage. With a greater population along the river and greater affluence, the loss of blood and treasure might easily be much larger.

Fantastic that a lone Panhandle outlaw might bring about such a condition? Not when said outlaw was Veck Sosna. Slade did not underestimate Sosna, his courage, shrewdness and persuasive powers. Let him really get started and the wronged and ignorant would flock to his banner. Such a catastrophe must be prevented at all costs.

How? At the moment Slade had not the slightest notion. However, the weak point in the arch was its keystone— Veck Sosna. Slade was not, as yet, combatting a condition but an individual. With Sosna disposed of, the fantastic scheme would dissolve. So all he had to do was put Sosna out of the picture. That was all, but past events more than intimated that the chore was a monumental one, even for El Halcón.

All of which passed through his mind as Amado Menendez discoursed on the matter. He reflected grimly that it was, in a way, a case of two minds that thought as one. For certainly Sosna must feel that El Halcón must be disposed of. Well, he'd have something to say about that.

The cantina was growing livelier, the tension easing as the various forms of alcohol imbibed by the gathering began getting in their licks. The naturally volatile spirits of the Mexicans were gaining the ascendancy and the cowhands from across the river didn't pay the whole business much mind, anyhow.

"But you can't blame folks for getting a bit jumpy," said Amado. "We've experienced that sort of thing before and didn't enjoy it. Flying lead doesn't play any favorites. Well,

54

reckon I'd better be moving around. Enjoy yourself, *amigo.*"

Slade determined to do just that. He felt he had a mite of relaxation and diversion coming to him; the past few days had been rather hectic.

Dolores came over and joined him. "Now what are you blushing about?" he teased.

"Darn it! when you look at me like that I can't help it," she replied.

"Want me to look differently?"

"No!" She smiled and dimpled, but was immediately serious.

"Did you get into more trouble today?" she asked. He shook his head.

"Fortunatly, no." Dolores looked doubtful.

"I'll tell you about it," he volunteered, and proceeded to do so.

"So you see, there was no trouble; just scared the boots off some gents."

She sighed and shook her head. "It appears you are dedicated to a life of violence," she said.

"I don't deliberately go looking for violence," he protested.

"I'm not so sure," she answered. "Sometimes I think you enjoy it. Why do you have to have such a terrible feud with the man Sosna you told me about?"

He gazed at her a moment, arrived at a decision.

"Not here," he said, "but tonight I'll tell you why. Then, I think you will understand."

"That's a promise?"

"It's a promise."

"I'm sure I'll understand," she said. "Not that I doubted for a moment that you are justified. Only I hate to think of you seeking vengeance for a wrong."

"I do not seek vengeance," he said gently. "Vengeance is a two-edged sword that cuts the heart of the wielder and leaves a wound that never heals. But sometimes violence is necessary if justice is to be done. Remember, with a whip of small cords, Our Lord scourged the money changers from the Temple."

Dolores bowed her shapely head. "I think I understand already," she said, her voice soft and low. "No matter what else you have to tell me, I understand."

"Thank you," he said simply.

She laughed gaily and sprang to her feet. "Let's dance," she said. "That is, if you don't think I'm forward in asking

55

you. After all, though, it's my business—that's what I'm here for, when I'm not doing something else."

"Like straightening out Amado's books," he smiled.

"And that really is a chore," she said. "The mess he can get things into! And his handwriting is like a barbed wire fence. Oh, yes, I can wash glasses, too. And that's not all I can do."

"To which I am ready and willing to bear witness," he said, falling in with her mood.

"And that," she replied, "will be enough of that; let's dance."

They had several dances together, then Slade went back to his table. He glanced at the clock over the bar. She would not be ready to leave for a couple of hours yet. He'd had all he wanted to drink and was growing a little weary of the noise. A walk in the night air wouldn't go bad.

He was ready to leave when Estevan came in. His dark, savage face was expressionless, but his black eyes were snapping. He glanced around, spotted Slade and came to the table. El Halcón motioned him to a chair and poured a glass of wine from the bottle Amado had placed on the table. Estevan nodded and downed half a glass at a gulp. Slade could see he was laboring under repressed excitement.

"Cápitan," he said, without preamble, "you will recall my friend who works in the cantina, El Toro, where the seamen drink, who spotted the man Sosna, your enemy? You will also recall that she said others were with him, to whom she paid scant attention. She did note their appearance, however. She just told me that two of those men are at the cantina at the moment; she pointed them out to me. I thought you should know."

Slade considered a moment. Undoubtedly the men in question were two of Sosna's followers. Which might mean that Sosna himself was not far off. There was a bare possibility that they might lead him to the outlaw leader. Worth trying, anyhow; nothing to lose.

"Grácias, Estevan," he said. "Would you show me the cantina?"

"I will certainly accompany you, Cápitan," the young vaquero replied. He tossed off the rest of his drink.

"You are ready, Cápitan?"

"Let's go," Slade replied.

Slade walked warily as they made their way through the narrow, crooked streets. Although it was quite late there

56

were still plenty of stray dogs and roaming cattle, horse-drawn vehicles and water carriers to impede their progress. Matamoros did most of its sleeping around midday when the sun was hot.

"What does *El Cápitan* plan to do?" Estevan asked, as they followed the curve of the river to the section of the town that, Slade knew, was of sinister reputation.

"I aim to loaf around in the cantina till that pair leaves," Slade explained. "Then I'll try to tail them and perhaps contact the big he-wolf of the pack. He may have arranged a meeting with them, for quite likely they are here to observe conditions and report to him."

"*Bueno!*" said Estevan. "No, no, *Cápitan*, I do not leave you," he interrupted as Slade started to speak. "Fear not that I will hamper you. I am *Indio* more than Spanish. I move as moves the shadow of the cloud and if I do not wish to be observed, I am not observed."

"Okay," Slade agreed. "We'll work together."

Now they could hear the moan and mutter of the river worrying its banks, for the Rio Grande was rising. There had been heavy rains in the Devil River and Pecos sections, and those tributaries were pouring flood waters into the parent stream. Abruptly Estevan pointed ahead.

"There is the cantina," he said, "it sits close to the water's edge."

Slade eyed the squat building, which had a dilapidated look, as they drew near. It did not appear overly well lighted.

"The men, where are they?" he asked his companion.

"They sit at a table across the room from the door, near a window," replied Estevan. "You will see them as we enter."

"We'll go straight to the bar without paying any attention to them," Slade said. "Perhaps we can observe them in the back bar mirror, if there is one, and see when they leave."

"There is a mirror," replied Estevan. "Here we are."

They stepped through the swinging doors. Slade shot a swift glance around. The room wasn't very big and was not overly crowded. Two hanging lamps, one over the bar, the other over the dance-floor, provided light. Across the room two men sat at a table, facing the door.

"They look our way," Estevan hissed over his shoulder.

57

NINE

THE MOVE WAS SO SWIFT, SO UTTERLY UNEXPECTED THAT
it very nearly caught El Halcón off balance. Almost but not
quite. Over went the heavy table, the two men behind it, guns
blazing. But even as they pulled trigger, Slade's arm sent
Estevan reeling out of line. In the same ripple of movement
he went sideways along the wall, both Colts gushing flame.

A bullet burned a streak along the top of his shoulder.
Another just grained the flesh of his left thigh. His slugs
thudded into the table top. In the dim light he could see almost nothing to shoot at.

Across the room the two guns tipped up. The reports sounded as one. The lamp chimneys flew to pieces,
the lights went out. Darkness swooped down like a thrown
blanket.

Pandemonium, hideous and absolute ensued. The yells
and curses of men, the screams of the dance-floor girls, and
the thudding of overturned furniture blended in a volcanic
uproar, through which Slade heard a crashing of glass and a
splintering of woodwork.

"Estevan, out!" he roared. "They went through the window!"

He whisked from the room, nearly taking the doors off
their hinges, and raced westward along a row of blank walls
—Estevan pounding after him—turned a corner, passed
another unlighted building and found himself in an alley
back of the still raving cantina.

There was no one in sight, but to his ears came a clatter
of hoofs fading eastward.

"Hold it!" he told the *vaquero*. "I guessed wrong. I thought
they'd go west, but they're headed east for the bridge.
River must be too high to ford."

Estevan was swearing in three languages. "*Nombre de
Dios! Maledicto! caramba!*" he bawled. "Now what *Cápitan?*"

"Back to Amado's place as fast as we can get there," Slade
replied. "The less we're mixed up down here the better."

"Come," said Estevan. He headed west at a fast pace,

circled around and reached the main part of the town, and slowed down.

"That was fast," Slade chuckled. "Sosna's men, all right, they think fast and act fast."

"But not so fast as El Halcón," Estevan said. *"Cápitan,* what does it mean?"

"One of two things," Slade answered. "Either they recognized me when I stepped in the door and figured I was coming after them or they spotted you when you were there, deduced that when you left you were going to fetch me and were all set for business when I came in. Hard to tell which; doesn't matter much either way, anyhow. They outsmarted me and very nearly got the jump on me."

Estevan grunted something derisive.

"I hope your lady friend didn't get hurt in the ruckus," Slade added.

Estevan shrugged. "I have others," he replied cheerfully. "Ha, here we are; a glass of wine will be good."

They sauntered in, located a table. Dolores came over at once, giving them a searching look.

"Now what have you been up to?" she asked. "You look like a couple of cats lapping a saucer of cream."

"The saucer got kicked over before we could lap it," Slade grinned.

"We went for a walk," Estevan interpolated. Dolores did not look convinced.

"Oh, well, I'll hear about it soon enough, that I'll wager," she said as she accepted a glass of wine.

She did hear, and shortly. A few minutes later a couple of cowhands bulged in, looking decidedly excited.

"Never saw such ruckus," one said loudly to companions at the bar. "Down in the rumhole, *El Toro,* on Rio Street. Bunch of hellions started a corpse and cartridge session. Shot the lights out, busted the windows, turned over the chairs and tables and knocked the swinging doors off the hinges. It was a whang-doddle for fair. Nope, nobody got cashed in. Some barked shins and bruised heads but nothing serious. What was it all about? Nobody seemed to know, or if they did they weren't saying. Nobody seemed to know the fellers mixed up in it. Some said there were only three or four. Sounded to me more like a dozen. All I know is that guns started blazing in every direction, then lights went out and Old Harry busted loose for fair. Pete and me got out of there as fast as we could. Everybody seemed to want to get out. Didn't know what to do when they did. Argument started on the street, and a couple of wrings. We left before the police showed up, which I reckon they did pronto. Folks in Brownsville must have heard it."

Dolores glared accusingly at her table companions. "If I let you out of my sight for five minutes you get into trouble," she said.

"*El Cápitan* gets not into trouble, it is others who get into trouble," said Estevan. "We broke no windows, turned over no chairs."

"But if you didn't start it, I'm greatly surprised," she retorted. "Walt, I'll be ready to leave in half an hour or so. You stay right here till I am."

"Yes, Ma'am," Slade replied meekly. Estevan chuckled.

"Ha!" he said. "To hear the great El Halcón take orders! It is indeed the novelty. Well, one must never think small of the powers of women; they command, and we must obey. More wine, *amigo*."

Slade was watchful and alert as they rode across the bridge and threaded the almost deserted streets of Brownsville. However, they reached the little white house without incident, stabled their horses and entered the living room.

"I'll make us some coffee," Dolores said. "Teresa must be sound asleep by now. Make yourself comfortable."

He proceeded to do so, stretching out in his favorite chair and rolling a cigarette.

Shortly she returned with the coffee and sat down on the floor beside him. She was silent while they drank the coffee, then she reminded him, "You promised to tell me tonight why you are so relentless in your pursuit of the man Sosna."

In answer, he drew something from a cunningly concealed secret pocket in his broad leather belt, and handed it to her. For a long moment she gazed at the famous silver star set on a silver circle, the feared and honored badge of the Texas Rangers.

"I see," she said. "It is not vengeance you seek, but justice."

"Yes," he replied. "The man Sosna is a ruthless killer from whom nobody, man or woman, is safe. It is in the service of decent people that I seek to run him down."

She touched the points of the star, one by one. "Courage, strength, service, justice, and fidelity," she said softly.

"Yes, those are the things it stands for," he said. "Now you understand."

"Yes, now I understand," she replied, with a sigh.

Very weary after a long and hard day, Slade slept late the following morning, for the coroner's jury would not sit on the bodies of the slain outlaws until afternoon, and there was no reason for him to arise early. Before dressing he reviewed the happening of the night before and pondered its possible significance.

Perhaps the two men had recognized him as El Halcón and had jumped at the conclusion that he was on their trail —the guilty flee when no man pursueth—nothing more than that.

Such was the logical conclusion, based to an extent at least on coincidence, something which El Halcón always regarded dubiously.

The disturbing fact existed that he was not sure. The two Sosna henchmen might well have been sent to Matamoros on a definite mission. Not surprising that they had visited the waterfront cantina, where they had been observed before. Quite likely they were cognizant of his association with Amado Menendez and Estevan. The vaquero had dropped in, engaged the girl in conversation and she had informed him of the presence of the two men whom she recalled being in the company of Veck Sosna, whose vivid personality had impressed her. Estevan was not an individual versed in the arts of duplicity. It was very possible that his expression and his unguarded glances had been noted by the unsavory pair. After talking with the girl he hurried out. For what? To inform El Halcón of their presence in the cantina. The way they sat facing the door and undoubtedly noting anybody who came in was significant. They were set for action when he entered.

So the alternate conclusion was a very unstable house of cards foundationed on sand, to badly scramble metaphors.

But Veck Sosna was not one to whom logic and reason could safely be applied. Better a witch's brew, a reading of tea leaves or the phases of the moon. So Slade's protracted ruminations had gotten him exactly nowhere. He yawned, chuckled, and sprang out of bed.

One thing was becoming more and more obvious; that Sosna had been hanging around Brownsville and Matamoros for quite a while. When he lost the outlaw's trail in Sonora it was evidently because Sosna had headed straight

61

for the Brownsville section, committing no depredations on the way which would denote his passing.

"And while I was chasing my tail through the Sonora mountains, he was here and getting established," he remarked, to his reflection in the mirror.

But where *was* Sosna? Was his hangout in Mexico or across the river? Slade didn't have the answer to either question, and on those answers the success or failure of his campaign against the outlaw and, incidentally, his own life, might well depend.

He descended to the living room. Teresa was out shopping, but Dolores was waiting to prepare his breakfast.

"Of course I didn't awaken you," she replied, to his apology for sleeping so late. "You had a hard day. And—night," she added, blushing and smiling. Immediately, however, she was serious.

"Walt," she said, "does Uncle Amado know you are a Ranger?"

"He does," Slade replied. "And so does Sheriff Calder here in Brownsville, and a few more folks who can be discreet."

"But to most people you are just a wanderer with a dubious reputation."

"Guess that's about the size of it," he admitted, with a smile.

"Which means that you are constantly exposed to danger." He shrugged his broad shoulders.

"The danger can bide," he replied cheerfully. "So far it hasn't done me much harm."

She shook her head dubiously and began making his breakfast.

Teresa arrived as they were sitting down to table. "What a scene of perfect domesticity," she said. "Early to bed and late to rise."

"I've been up for more than an hour," Dolores replied, indignantly.

"Not a bad idea," said Teresa, "although you always look charming, even early in the morning." She crinkled her eyes at Slade, who smiled. Dolores ignored them both.

The inquest was a formality, nothing more. Plant 'em, said the jury. They got just what was coming to them.

"And now what?" Sheriff Calder asked, as he and Slade sat together over a drink.

"I'll be darned if I know," the Ranger admitted. "I've not the slightest idea where Sosna is, nor what he has in mind."

"Do you think he really plans to foment an uprising on the other side of the river?"

"I wouldn't put it past him," Slade replied. "There's some ominous talk going on south of the Rio Grande. And he's evidently been here longer than I supposed. With discontent existing all along the Border, all that's needed to start real trouble is a leader able to attract the discontented with flowery promises. Sosna and his men are not the ordinary brush-popping outlaw type. As I said, he's a person with brain power and magnetism, and the sort of a following he always manages to get together is far from stupid. I hesitate to predict one way or the other. Anyhow, with Sosna alive and kicking we're due for trouble of some kind. Of one thing you can be sure for certain, if he does start an incipient revolution, he won't be leading a poorly armed rabble as did Cartinas and others of his calibre, but a well equipped, organized and hard hitting striking force that may even give *El Presidente* cause for concern. At first, I'd say, he'll only have loot in mind, but once let him realize his potential and he may get loftier notions. Success breeds ambition and ambition presupposes further success. No telling where he might end up. A Sosna regime south of the Border would be something to reckon with."

"Sounds fantastic," commented the sheriff.

"Yes, it does," Slade conceded, "but it is not as fantastic as it sounds. The country is misgoverned and sooner or later the present government will fall. What succeeds it will be of vital importance to Texas, and to all America for that matter."

He paused, his eyes gazing southward, in them a look of vision.

"The time will come," he said slowly, "that a leader will arise, a man of the people, who will lead the people to liberty and well being. There will be turmoil and bloodshed and misunderstanding, but out of these will come a new, prosperous and strong Mexico that will stand shoulder to shoulder with America in time of trouble."

Gazing at him, Sheriff Calder felt that here was more than a prediction. Here was a true vision of things to come. The sheriff was right.

La Cucaracha! La Cucaracha! Vive Villa!

TEN

"WELL," SLADE SAID, SETTING ASIDE HIS EMPTY GLASS, "I think I'll amble over to Matamoros and find out if Amado has learned anything. That ruckus last night may have developed some ramifications that could be interesting. Be seeing you."

Heavy with thought, Slade rode slowly across the bridge. He visited with Amado Menendez, but the conference was barren of results.

"They're close-mouthed at that cantina on Rio Street," Amado said. "Nobody knows anything about what happened there last night. Or if they do they're not admitting it. Peaceful enough down there now. Nothing has been seen of your *amigo*, Sosna."

"Looks like the hellion may have hunted cover for a while," Slade replied. "But," he added morosely, "I'm willing to wager that he'll cut loose somewhere before long."

At just about that moment, Walt Slade was being proved no mean prophet.

The Hidalgo bank was not a large bank, but because the town serviced a prosperous section, as well as the Mexican town of Reynosa across the river, there was usually plenty of money in its massive vault. The town had been raided by bandits more than once in the past, because of which the tellers, cashier and other officials were very much on the alert against possible robbery. All were armed, as was a watchful guard who paced back and forth in the small lobby.

There was a back door to the building, but it was of ponderous oak and always locked. The lock, although old-fashioned and clumsy looking, was strong. There was little chance of anybody crashing that door.

It was near closing time and the money in the cages was being transferred to the vault.

Up the street on which the bank fronted, from the east, rode half a dozen horsemen. And at the same time, an equal number rode in from the west. Each group was but a hundred feet from the bank when one of the riders let out a yell of alarm. The groups jerked their mounts to a halt and went for their guns. The street fairly exploded to a bellow of sixshooters.

One of the first group fell to the ground and lay still, the reins of his horse looped about his wrist. A moment later one of the opposite group fell. Strange to say, the reins of *his* mount were also looped about his wrist. Items not noticed in the excitement. Yells, curses, the booming of guns filled the air. To all appearances it was a corpse and cartridge session between two rival outfits.

The bank officials, not unnaturally, ran to the front window and peered out cautiously as the battle continued amid yelps of pain and louder shouting. Citizens on the street discreetly retired indoors.

The bankers, absorbed in the hectic scene, did not hear the turning of a key in the back-door lock, nor the slight click as the bolt slid back. Their first intimation that they had company was when a voice with a singular bell-tone quality rang out, "Elevate! You're covered!"

The bankers whirled around and stared into three gun muzzles. The guard made the mistake of grabbing for his iron.

The tallest of the three men shot him through the heart.

"Anyone else?" he asked. "All right, over in the corner, face the wall."

The raging bankers obeyed; there was nothing else to do. The tall man held his gun on them while his companions rushed back behind the grilling and into the vault, swiftly transferring its contents into canvas sacks they carried.

"Okay," one called.

"Better stay right where you are, gentlemen," said the tall gunman. He backed behind the grilling, dodged swiftly out the back door. An instant later three evenly spaced shots sounded behind the building.

The shooting in the street abruptly ceased. The "dead" men sprang to their feet and forked their horses. Both groups raced east out of town. Ahead, the three robbers were already sifting sand.

The wrathful and demoralized bankers stormed into the street. It was some minutes before they could make the bewildered crowd streaming from shops and residences understand what had happened. A horseman raced to Edinburgh, the county seat of Hidalgo County, and contacted the sheriff, who in turn sent a telegram to Sheriff Calder telling him to be on the lookout for a dozen bank robbers headed his way.

"I'll be on the lookout for them, but I won't see them," Calder snorted to Deputy Bowles. He saddled his horse and galloped across the bridge to confer with Walt Slade, whom he found in Amado's cantina.

"Didn't get any details," he said. "Just know they robbed the bank and headed this way. I suppose John Perkins of Hidalgo County will show up here after a while, and we'll get the lowdown."

"The Sosna bunch, all right, you can bet on that," Slade said.

"Think I'd better get a posse together and ride west on the chance of intercepting the devils?" Calder asked.

"If you feel the need of the exercise; otherwise I'd advise you to sit tight until we learn what really happened," Slade replied. "Will take your Hidalgo County sheriff some time to get here."

"Makes sense," grunted Calder. "Let us drink."

Dolores was in the back room working on the books. Slade went in and told her what had happened.

"No, I'm not riding after bank robbers tonight," he assured her. "I'll be here to accompany you home." He returned to the sheriff, who was discussing a drink with Amado. They talked for a while and then Calder rode back to his office.

"I'll be there around midnight," Slade promised. "You're not apt to learn anything before then."

Slade remained in the cantina for a while, after stabling Shadow, then walked around the town a bit. Out of curiosity he visited the cantina on Rio Street. Nobody paid him any attention and he sized up the crowd as ordinary, including quite a number of seamen. He went back to Amado's place for a word with Dolores, and a little later rode across the bridge to the sheriff's office.

It was well past midnight when the Hidalgo sheriff and his posse arrived, after a tiresome and fruitless ride. The posse men went in search of liquid refreshment and something to eat. Perkins remained with Calder and Slade and immediately launched into a detailed account of the robbery and murder.

"It was a plumb new one," he concluded. "I've heard of all sorts, supposed-to-be prospectors coming in with a big sack of nuggets to distract attention, and such, but staging a phony gun fight in the street was a plumb new wrinkle.

"Here's the key they used to open the back door," he added, producing it from his pocket and handing it to Sheriff Calder, who examined it and passed it to Slade. The Ranger turned it over in his slim fingers.

It was new and shiny and bore the marks of a file.

"The Sosna touch," he said to Calder. "He's a whizzer at locks, and anything else he turned his hand to, for that matter. Scouted the building and its surroundings, took a wax impression of the keyhole and had no trouble figuring out just the key needed to open the door. Yes, Sosna, all right."

"Sosna?" Perkins remarked interrogatively. Slade nodded to Calder, who obliged with a lurid account of the Panhandle outlaw leader and his doings. Sheriff Perkins swore in weary disgust.

"So it looks like we've got real trouble on our hands," he said.

"Yep, looks that way," Calder agreed cheerfully, adding, with a nod at Slade, "But I've a notion El Halcón will take care of it for us, sooner or later."

Sheriff Perkins jumped in his chair and stared at Slade. "El Halcón!" he repeated. "Seems I've heard about you, son. Don't folks say that—"

"That I'm an owlhoot too smart to get caught," Slade smilingly interrupted.

"Well—well—" sputtered the bewildered sheriff.

"Don't let 'it bother you, John," Calder chuckled. "I'll vouch for him."

Sheriff Perkins nodded, and studied Slade. "From what I've heard tell of you, I wouldn't be surprised if you do give the side-winder his comeuppance," he conceded. "Sorta on the prod against him, eh?"

"Well, he's tried to kill me a few times," Slade equivocated, leaving the sheriff to draw his own conclusions.

"That does get a feller sorta riled," Perkins admitted. "Well, good luck to you, and good hunting."

"Thank you," Slade replied. "And now suppose we ride over to Matamoros for a drink and something to eat. I have to meet a friend there later."

"Suits me," said Calder.

"A good notion," agreed Perkins. "I'm starved. The boys

can look after themselves for a while and we'll spend the night here."

After they reached the cantina and gave their orders to a waiter, Slade repaired to the back room for a word with Dolores, leaving the two sheriffs at a table together.

"I can't understand that young feller," Perkins complained.

"Well, you've got plenty of company," Calder replied dryly. "But I'll tell you one thing, he's a man to ride the river with."

"I've a notion you're right," Perkins said with nodded agreement to the highest compliment the rangeland can pay.

"How much did they get?" Slade asked, when he returned to the table.

"Thirty-five thousand and better," Perkins replied. "A nice haul."

"Yes, very nice," Slade agreed. "*Señor* Sosna will feel that he sort of evened up for the Bravo debacle," he added to Calder.

"Let me tell you about that one," Calder said. His account of the frustrated robbery of the river steamer and the part Slade played lost nothing in the telling. In fact, El Halcón felt that it gained a mite. But before he could protest, Calder was detailing, with equal vividness, the attempt to drygulch the posse on the river trail. Perkins shook his head.

"No wonder you swear by him," he said. "Son, I hope you see fit to coil your twine in this section. Why don't you get Tom to sign you on as a deputy? I'm sure he could fix it with the Commissioners."

"Not a bad notion, I'll think on it," Slade replied seriously. Calder chuckled.

"Better than mavericking around and always taking the chance of getting into serious trouble," Perkins insisted. "Do think on it."

Their dinner arrived and for a while conversation languished. Which gave Slade a chance to do a little serious thinking. Looked like Sosna was well on the way to amass a hefty chunk of capital for whatever venture he might have in mind. Which was disturbing. With what he had gathered in the course of his raids across Mexico, he must be pretty well heeled and ready to further any hare-brained scheme that would occur to him. Although, Slade admitted to him-

68

self, hare-brained was not exactly the proper descriptive adjective to apply to Veck Sosna.

The two sheriffs were old cronies and were conversing animatedly. Slade found their reminiscenses interesting and entertaining. Meanwhile he was doing some hard thinking. Gradually he evolved a plan he believed might work. He estimated the distance the outlaws would have to cover to reach the ford, and by now he was firmly convinced that Sosna's real headquarters was somewhere south of the Rio Grande and not in Texas, although he might have a temporary hole-up on the north side of the stream.

He felt sure the band would not follow the main trail, which ran through the town of Pharr, three miles to the north of Hidalgo to reach the ford. To do so they would risk possible interception. But there were trails through the brush country to the north, for those who knew them. It would be much the longer route but he was certain Sosna would take it, reaching the vicinity of the ford somewhere around or before daybreak. He did not believe the outlaws would risk the ford during the hours of darkness. The river, though not quite so swollen as the night before, was still a bit high, and daylight would be needed to safely negotiate the crossing.

"Tom," he said abruptly, "I'm going to play a hunch, if you fellows will string along with me."

"Anything you say goes," Calder instantly replied. Sheriff Perkins nodded agreement.

"What do you want us to do?" Calder asked.

"I want you to head back to Brownsville and round up Perkins's posse. They are in Cameron County, or course, so swear everybody in as special deputies; that will give them all the lawful authority they need. Then ride to that bend just east of the trail, where we had the ruckus with the hellions the other day. Hole up there and wait. I feel confident that around daybreak the hellions will show. With good luck you might be able to bag the whole bunch."

"By gosh! that sounds good," said Calder. "We'll do it. You're not coming with us?" Slade shook his head.

"I'm going to where I have no business to be, the south end of the ford, on Mexican soil; I believe I'm justified in fracturing International Law a mite. I think I'll be able to stop any of the devils that escape from crossing."

"You'll be taking a chance," Calder protested. "Best as

I remember, there's no cover on the south bank of the river; you'll be right out in the open."

"So will they," Slade replied. "Anyhow, I'll risk it. Only hope a detachment of *rurales* don't come along and drop a loop on me. Don't think there's much danger of that happening, though. Everything understood?"

"All hunky-dory," said Calder, rising to his feet. "Come on, John, we got things to do." They hurried out.

Estevan was at the bar, talking to Amado. Slade sauntered over and joined them.

"Do me a favor, *amigo*?" he asked of the *vaquero*.

"Of a certainty, *Cápitan*," was the instant reply. "Who do you wish killed?"

"Not quite that serious," Slade smiled. "I'd like for you to ride home with Dolores tonight; I'll be detained."

"It will be the great pleasure," Estevan promised.

"Grácias," Slade replied, and headed for the back room.

"Estevan will ride across the bridge with you tonight," he told the girl. "I have a little chore to attend to; see you later."

Her eyes were dark with apprehension, but she did not seek to dissuade him. She merely clung to him a moment.

"Please be careful," she begged.

"I will," he promised. He kissed her lightly and left the room. Her eyes followed his tall form through the door.

"At this rate, my hair will soon be snow-white," she told the books on the table.

ELEVEN

SLADE RODE WEST AT A LEISURELY PACE, for he had plenty of time if things worked out per schedule. Reaching the head of the ford, he sat for a moment gazing across the river, which was silvered by the light of the waning moon; the water was not very high, not enough to deter anybody really anxious to cross. He led Shadow back a little distance down the trail, where he would be safe from flying lead, flipped the bit out and left him to graze. Returning to the ford, he rolled a cigarette, sat down and schooled himself to patience; it still lacked a while till dawn.

Gradually the sky grayed, the east flushed rose and pink. The stars turned from gold to silver, dwindled to needle-points of steel and winked out. The glow in the east strengthened, birds began to chirp. The rose and pink deepened to crimson flecked with ruddy gold. A shaft of light shot upward, reached the zenith, fell earthward. The flaming rim of the sun appeared, a little wind shook down a myriad of dew from the blades of grass, and it was day.

Slade knew that his position was not the best, outlined as he would be in the blaze of sunlight, but there was no help for it. Nowhere was there any cover. He made sure the mechanism of his Winchester was in perfect order, rolled another cigarette.

On the north bank of the stream there was no sign of life. The chaparral stood stiffly erect, its points glittering in the sun bath, devoid of movement. Evidently the posse was under cover.

To the west of the ford, as to the east, the trail curved sharply through the chaparral. And where it curved, Slade fixed his gaze. Still nothing moved, no sound save the ripple of the river broke the silence.

Then as if jerked forward by invisible strings, a tight group of riders, more than a dozen in all, bulged around the bend and sped toward the ford. Slade could not hear Sheriff Calder's shout of, "Elevate! You're covered!" but he saw

71

the puffs of smoke mushroom from the group, as they jerked their mounts to a slithering halt. And the answering puffs from the brush. A moment later the crackle of the reports reached him. He held his rifle at the ready, his eyes fixed on the riders sitting their rearing horses. He saw men fall, other lurch and sway. It was as if he had a front seat at a stage performance.

Then, just as he expected, a rider detached from the swirling group, sped to the ford and sent his mount into the water. Slade raised the rifle, clamped the butt against his shoulder. His eyes glanced along the sights and he squeezed the trigger.

The rider whirled from his saddle, struck the water below the ford and vanished. A second horseman charged toward the river's edge. Slade shifted the rifle barrel a fraction. Two riderless horses plunged across the river. A third tried it, whirled his mount as a slug sent his hat spinning through the air. That was all. No others dared face that unerring rifle.

The possemen were streaming from the brush, closing the distance, shooting as fast as they could pull trigger. Slade saw the remaining outlaws swerve their horses, doubtless at a word of command, and hightail to the growth. One didn't quite make it and fell in the middle of the trail. The others dashed on, shooting over their shoulders.

Slade held his fire; he did not dare shoot toward the wild and intermingled battle there on the trail. He saw the sheriff's men turn and dash back the way they had come. A moment later they reappeared, mounted, and sped after the fleeing owlhoots. One lingered, waving and beckoning. Slade waved back and he skalleyhooted after the others.

Slade stayed right where he was. He grounded his rifle and rolled a cigarette. He had no intention of riding across the river. If some of the outlaws circled around and back to the ford, he could find himself at an unpleasant disadvantage in the middle of the stream.

The two outlaw horses had reached the bank and were trying to gaze. He approached them without difficulty, removed the rigs and left them to their own devices. Returning, he again took up his position at the head of the ford.

An hour passed slowly, part of another, and then horsemen reappeared from the brush, riding slowly. They waved their hands to him. Slade retrieved Shadow and put him to the water. The river was still a bit high, but he had no difficulty negotiating the crossing. Sheriff Calder bellowed a greeting.

"Did for seven of the blankety-blanks," he whooped. "And you got two. Nine altogether, not a bad bag. The rest got away; we lost 'em in the brush."

"And Sosna one of those that got away, I suppose," Slade replied, as Shadow snorted his way to dry land.

"Reckon so," agreed the sheriff. "A big tall jigger who 'peared to be directing things was one of 'em that went into the brush. Yep, guess that was him."

"Anybody badly hurt?" Slade asked.

"Oh, two or three of the boys got airholes in their hides, nothing too bad, I figure. We got part of the bank money back, too. Found a saddle pouch stuffed with it, about half, I'd say. Yes, we didn't do so bad, thanks to you."

Slade secured his medicants from his saddle pouches and went to work on the injured, bandaging a couple of punctured thighs, a hole through a shoulder and a bullet gashed cheek.

"Caught 'em off balance and they didn't shoot so good," observed Calder. "Last thing they expected to happen, I figure. We had pretty good cover, too. Didn't come out till they showed signs of hightailing. Say, that was some shooting you did; it's a good six hundred yards."

"Good shooting light, with the sun beating down on them as it was," Slade said, deprecating his marksmanship. "Let's have a look at the carcasses."

He was not at all surprised to find that Sosna was among the missing.

"I sometimes wonder if the bullet is run that can down the hellion," he remarked morosely. "He wasn't one of the pair that went into the river, of that I'm certain. I'd hoped he'd try to make it across. Rather thought he would, but I guess he was to smart to try it. He sizes up a situation in a flash, and never panics."

"You'll get him, sooner or later," the sheriff predicted cheerfully. "Anyhow, his bunch is sure getting thinned out. An even dozen already that we can account for."

"But it won't take him long to round up replacements," Slade said. "Until he is accounted for, the chore isn't half done. Well, I've a notion today gave him a mite of a jolt. About half the money recovered, you say? He still made a

73

pretty good haul. I imagine he was packing the other half."

"Quite likely," agreed Calder, "but his take is a darn sight less than he figured it to be."

Sheriff Perkins came out to enthusiastically shower Slade with congratulations on the success of his maneuver.

"Even a Ranger couldn't have done a better chore," he declared. Sheriff Calder chuckled. Slade smiled.

The dead outlaws' horses were rounded up, the bodies roped to the saddles. The posse made a triumphant entry into Brownsville.

A doctor was called to examine the wounded. He complimented Slade on the way he had cared for the injuries.

"You've got the making of a fine surgeon," he said. "The hands and everything. Why can't you young fellows put your natural talents to use?"

Which caused Sheriff Calder to chuckle again.

After the bodies were disposed of, the sheriffs and the possemen went to bed. Slade repaired to the house on Jackson Street, where he found Dolores sitting up.

"Of course I didn't go to bed," she said. "How could I?"

"Come and get your breakfast, or whatever you want to call it," Teresa said from the kitchen.

After he had finished eating, she said, "And now upstairs with both of you. You look as if you were dead on your feet.

"I'm going out for a while," she added pointedly.

Slade grinned. Dolores made a face at her.

It was in a fairly satisfied frame of mind that Slade went to sleep. Although the outlaw leader escaped, he felt that he had dealt Sosna a body blow that might well shake his confidence. However, he did not for a moment think that the shrewd and salty hellion would pull out of the section or desist from whatever scheme he had in mind. That wouldn't be Veck Sosna.

When Slade dropped in at the sheriff's office, shortly after sunset, he found that official gazing at a scattering of odds and ends and a heap of money on his desk.

"From those hellions' pockets," he explained. "What shall I do with the *dinero*? I suppose it should go into the county treasury or to the bank, or something."

"Wouldn't be surprised if the boys of the posse could use

74

it, especially the wounded," Slade replied. "They won't be able to work much for a few days."

"A notion," agreed the sheriff. He shoved a handful of silver to one side.

"That for the treasury," he said. "Now my official conscience is clear. John will be in shortly and I'll give the rest to him to divide."

While waiting for Perkins to show up, Slade examined the trinkets from the outlaws' pockets but found nothing of significance.

"Their sort never pack anything that might tie them up with something," he said. "Count on Sosna to make sure of that."

When Sheriff Perkins arrived, a little while later, Calder handed the money to him, repeating Slade's suggestion.

"Fine!" he said. "Will give the boys a nice bust in town; we don't figure to head back to Edinburgh till tomorrow morning."

He started to pocket the money, hesitated, glanced questioningly at Slade. The Ranger smilingly shook his head.

"Okay, if that's the way you feel about it," Perkins said. "But I figure you really earned every dadburned cent of it."

Slade laughed, and changed the subject.

"Don't suppose anybody recalled anything about those devils?"

"If they did they wouldn't admit it," the sheriff answered. "Frankly, I don't think anybody did; they 'pear to be plumb strangers to the section."

"From the looks of them, I've a notion they were all members of his Panhandle outfit, the Comancheros," Slade said, thoughtfully. "I wonder how many of the hellions he persuaded to come down here, anyhow?"

"Looked to me to have Indian blood, all of them," Perkins commented.

"Most of them do have, Comanche," Slade replied.

"And the Comanches are ripsnorters for fair," grunted Calder. "Well, at the rate they're being knocked off, he'll hafta rattle his hocks to keep his corral full."

"He will," Slade predicted.

"By the way," said Perkins, "I was telling the boys about that place across the river we visited last night. They sort of hanker to drop over there. Okay? I'll round them up."

It was a motley appearing crew that crossed the bridge to Matamoros. One had his cheek crisscrossed with court plaster, another an arm in a sling. Two more limped badly but refused to be left behind.

"What is it, invasion or fugitives from the field of battle?" Amado chuckled, as they filed into *La Luz* and were introduced. "Be that as it may, the *amigos* of El Halcón are always welcome. First drink is on the house."

"He's a real *hombre*, all right," Perkins declared. "Say, that black-haired girl with the blue eyes is something!"

"Hands off," warned Calder. "That's Slade's friend."

"Us old fellers never have a chance," the Hidalgo sheriff lamented.

"Old!" snorted Calder. "You ain't forty yet. Wait till you're my age and then you can talk."

Perkins shook his head dubiously, but later, on the dance-floor, he appeared amply consoled by a little *señorita* with laughing eyes and a roguish smile.

Estevan strolled in, drew Slade aside and spoke in low tones, "This evening, just after sundown, men forded the river. A wandering *pastor* who is my *amigo* told me that they were six in number, and that one was very tall. They rode west. He was standing in a thicket some distance away and did not approach."

"Lucky he didn't," Slade said. "They might well have murdered him out of pure devilishness, or because they didn't wish to be noticed."

Privately, he believed that the *pastor* in question had been planted where he was by Estevan to keep a watch on the ford.

"*Gracias, amigo,*" he said, "it may prove of value."

Slade felt that it would; for in his opinion, it confirmed his suspicion that Sosna had his real headquarters south of the river. A nebulous plan was forming in his mind, which he determined to put into effect once he got the details satisfactorily ironed out.

The evening passed pleasantly and everybody had a good time. Even the wounded men grew quite hilarious and forgot their injuries. Sheriff Perkins danced with nearly every girl on the floor, including Dolores. It was into the morning hours when they decided to call it a night.

Dolores quit early and rode across the bridge with them. "I'm well protected tonight," she whispered to Slade. "Your friend the sheriff, whom you said is lonely, is very nice. And the way he sang your praises!"

"I fear he grossly exaggerates," Slade said, with a smile.

"He struck me as being very sincere," she countered. "Out of wine cometh truth."

'Or sometimes snakes, or so I've been told," he chuckled.

"You're impossible!"

TWELVE

Slade went to bed feeling that the night had not been wasted. He figured himself justified in his belief that *La Luz* was a clearing house for Border information. The word Estevan brought him apparently substantiated his deduction that Sosna had his hangout somewhere in Mexico, and it provided the first inkling as to where the hangout might be. The six men rode west, according to Estevan's informant. So it was logical to think that their destination was somewhere west of Matamoros, quite likely not far off. Perhaps in the rugged foothills of the great central plateau and the Sierra Madres, which began no great distance from the flat coastal plain where Matamoros lay. Well, it was up to him to find out. But how? That was the unanswered question.

He awoke, some hours later, with the resolution strengthened, but with the "how" still unanswered. He could hardly go riding blithely along the Camino Trail hoping that opportunity would suddenly and graciously appear. That would be decidedly a negative approach and not likely to produce results.

It is a truism that big things grow from small things, and that all things, large or small, are made up of trifles. So what seemed at first glance of scant significance turned out to be highly important.

The Mexican State of Tamaulipas was rich in oil, fine woods and succulent wild fruits. Ships from every land were constantly arriving at its ports. Some of these made their way up the Rio Grande to Brownsville and beyond. And some, Slade knew, were not above a little genteel smuggling to bolster the emoluments of legitimate trade.

He had ridden to Matamoros and had wandered onto the wharf back of Amado's cantina, where he had frustrated Sosna's attempt to rob the Bravo's safe.

A steamer moored there interested him. She was a tramp, all right, her funnel streaked, her woodwork dilapidated.

But she looked staunch enough, her hull plates painted against rust. He surveyed her idly, his thoughts elsewhere. Suddenly he noticed something that would very likely have been overlooked by anyone who lacked El Halcón's eyesight. Two thin lines of jointure, about ten feet apart, ran from just below the deck to almost the waterline. They appeared to have been recently painted over, with care. His gaze traveled across the space between them where they ended above the waterline. Yes, the thing was undoubtedly hinged; a section of the vessel's side could be let down to form a broad gangplank.

Nothing strictly original about that, but why the apparent effort to make the fact unnoticeable? Slade's black brows drew together until the concentration furrow was deep between them.

A surly looking deckhand was leaning over the rail. A short nod was his answer to Slade's greeting.

"What you packing this trip?" the Ranger asked casually.

The man shot him a suspicious glance, seemed to hesitate. "We're going up the river to pick up a cargo of hides and tallow," he replied ungraciously. Slade nodded and walked away.

Smoke was pouring from the ship's funnel; evidently she was getting up steam with the intention of pulling away soon. Slade glanced back at her and suddenly quickened his pace. He hurried to the stable and got the rig on Shadow.

"Horse," he said, "I'm playing a hunch. Maybe we're just going on a fool's errand, but somehow I don't think we are. That old tub isn't going to load hides and tallow; she's going to load stock. Smuggling, of course, is none of our business—that's up to the Customs people—but smuggling attended by robbery and possible killings on Texas soil *is* some of our business. Let's go!"

Half an hour later he had crossed the bridge, passed through Brownsville and was riding swiftly along the trail that ran not far from the river bank.

Passing the ford, he rode on for a couple of miles, drew rein at a suitable spot from which he could see unobserved, and settled himself to wait. He knew that farther on were cattle and sheep ranches, especially the latter; sheep throve on the hill pastures that were not the best for cows.

It proved a tedious wait, but after an hour or so, it paid off. The old tramp came chugging up the stream, her propeller swirling the yellow water. Slade noted quite a few men loitering about her deck, a rather large crew for so small a ship.

"She packs contraband, all right," he told Shadow. "I think the hunch is a straight one."

Shadow snorted resignedly and masticated a mesquite pod he had filched from the nearby growth.

Slade let the steamer get well ahead before he rode on; sharp eyes on her deck might notice a rider trailing her. That is if she was up to something that would not bear scrutiny, which he was confident now that she was. If so, things ought to happen before so very long.

But as the afternoon waned and the vessel kept chow-chowing on her way, he began to wonder uneasily if he'd guessed wrong. Was beginning to look a little that way.

As the sun sank behind the ramparts of the Sierra Madres and shadows encroached on the trail, he closed the distance quite a bit, satisfied he could no longer be observed from the deck.

Suddenly the vessel veered, slanting purposefully to the right. Ahead the growth thickened; Slade rode on, reached a point where it thinned a little, abruptly ended, and resumed again a dozen yards or so to the west. The opening appeared to extend northward up a gentle incline. Slade pulled to a halt and sat watching.

A moment later the steamer bumped against the bank. A chain rattled through a hawsehole, the anchor chunked into the mud and the little ship hung motionless.

A windlass clanked, there was a creaking sound and the hinged section of the vessel's side slowly lowered until its upper portion rested on the bank, providing a wide and serviceable gangplank.

"Just as I figured," Slade whispered to Shadow, "they're all set to load, and their cargo will come down through that gap in the brush. Must be a trail over there. Now what to do?"

He pondered the question a moment. "We're going up that trail and see what it leads to," he told the horse. "Waiting here until something happens may not be such a good notion."

He urged his mount into the brush, which here was not so thick as farther back, and sent him slowly up the rise for a couple of hundred yards. Then he turned sharply west. A few minutes later he reached the opening in the chaparral. As he predicted, there was a trail, a narrow and little used trail that very likely had once been an Indian track. Pausing a moment to peer and listen, he entered the trail and rode on up the gentle slope, very slowly and very much on the alert.

For something less than a quarter of a mile the trail continued, gradually leveling off. It reached what was evidently the crest of the low rise. Slade drew rein and gazed down the opposite shallow sag.

Directly below was a heavily grassed pasture, hemmed on the north, at no great distance, by a belt of growth, and extending indefinitely to the west. Huddled together a couple of hundred yards from the bottom of the sag were two hundred or more sheep. A fire glowed and around it moved the figures of the two *pastors* who guarded the woolies against wolves, coyotes and other predatory critters. Slade was beginning to get the drift of things.

He started to ride down and say a word of warning to the shepherds, then decided to wait until the light dimmed a little more and he would be less likely to be observed by possible watching eyes as he crossed the level ground. Later he was to regret that decision.

The flame of the sunset sky paled. The lovely blue dusk sifted down from the hilltops like impalpable dust. Slade started to descend the slope.

But as his hand tightened on the reins a burst of gunfire sounded from the nearby brush. The two *pastors* fell like sacks of old clothes, to lie motionless.

Slade swore bitterly under his breath; his hesitancy had cost two lives. But he knew that if he had ridden across the open space before the light faded, he would very likely be one with the dead shepherds on the ground.

From the chaparral rode half a dozen men, grotesque, distorted in the deepening gloom. Slade saw them start the flock moving. He turned Shadow and rode swiftly back down the trail. Nearing the river's edge, he turned his mount into the brush and circled around until he reached his former position on the main trail at the edge of the growth, and waited.

"We'll see if we can't even the score for those two poor devils," he breathed to Shadow.

Lanterns flickered on the ship's deck and inside the yawning opening in her side. Two deckhands came down the gangplank and stationed themselves on either side. Slade waited, tense and watchful.

But a little time passed before he heard the bleat of the coming sheep. He drew both guns, settled himself firmly in the saddle. He would be putting himself at a disadvantage, but he was a law enforcement officer, subject to the stern code of the Rangers; he must give the ruthless devils a chance to surrender.

The beam of a searchlight blazed forth, focused on the gangplank and the trail through the brush. That would help. He would be in the shadow, the wide-loopers outlined in the glare. Now the odds wouldn't be so lopsided. Still, six to one, plus possible assistance from the ship, was not comfortable.

The first of the protesting sheep came into view, streamed across the trail toward the gangplank. The leaders milled, hesitated. Urged on by the two deckhands, some scattered up the plank and vanished into the ship's hold. Perhaps a score had been loaded when the outlaws showed behind the others. Slade's pulses leaped as he recognized the tall, flashing-eyed foremost rider. His hunch had been a straight one; Sosna and his bunch! He trained one gun on the Comanchero leader. His voice rang out, "Up! You're covered!"

And Sosna did the unexpected. He went sideways from the saddle, gun blazing, even as Slade pulled the trigger. Livid with fury, El Halcón knew he had missed. He shot with both hands, saw a man fall, another. Answering bullets stormed through the brush, but he was hidden from view and none found a mark. He strained his eyes for a glimpse of Sosna.

The searchlight snapped off. The forms of the outlaws were but shifting shadows at which Slade fired again and again. Then the bell tones of Sosna's voice rang out. There was a clattering of hoofs, drumming westward. Slade sent Shadow surging forward, and instantly the black horse was engulfed by the terrified sheep.

It was like fighting a flour sack or a snow bank. Sheep were knocked aside, others went down. Shadow slipped on a bleating wooly body, stumbled, nearly fell, floundered, and ended up facing the wrong way.

Slade gave up; the outlaws now had a head start and would vanish into the brush somewhere before he could hope to sight them. The odds were still four to one, and now the element of possible surprise and ambush would be on their side.

The steamer's funnel was roaring, the windlass clanking frantically. The captain was swinging her around, heedless of the gaping opening in his ship's side just above the water line. Slade stuffed fresh cartridges into his empty guns.

A shot rang out from the vessel's deck; the slug fanned the Ranger's face. He emptied both guns at the retreating steamer. A yell of pain echoed the reports, and a torrent of curses. Then ship and crew vanished into the mist rising from the water, the windlass still clanking, the funnel booming. Away she went, down river like a coyote with its tail a-fire.

Disgustedly Slade again reloaded his guns. He debated racing the steamer to Brownsville and having her intercepted. What was the use! He hadn't a thing on her. Long before she reached the town, the sheep would be tossed overboard and there would not be a scintilla of evidence that would stand up in court.

"Well, from the way one of the hellions aboard her yelped, I've a notion he isn't feeling too good right now," he growled to Shadow. "Let's see what we bagged. I think we made it fifty-fifty for those poor devils of *pastors*."

There were two dead men on the river bank, typical Sosna followers, Slade concluded. Their pockets revealed nothing of interest. The horses they rode were nowhere in sight; evidently they had skalleyhooted after the others.

The sheep, docile creatures, had quieted and were nosing about nibbling grass; they would make out until they were picked up.

Against the very unlikely possibility that one of the shepherds might have been only wounded, Slade rode back to the pasture below the sag, and found nothing but death. He had no notion where their employer might live and was in no mood to ride all over Texas endeavoring to locate him. Sheriff Calder could ride out and attend to that chore. With a final glance around, he headed for Brownsville.

Well, it hadn't been too bad a night, he reflected. He had put another crimp in *Señor* Sosna's activities. But, as usual, Sosna himself got in the clear. If he didn't get a break he made one, Slade grudgingly admitted. His mind worked with the smooth efficiency of an oiled mechanism; and brain and body synchronized perfectly. But perhaps the next time—

Slade let Shadow take his time on the return trip and it

was past midnight when he reached Brownsville. Playing a hunch, he rode straight to the sheriff's office, where a light burned. Calder was dozing comfortably in his chair.

"Oh, sure I waited up for you," he said, yawning and rubbing his eyes. "I figured you'd amble in sooner or later with something to tell me. All right, let's have it."

Slade recounted his adventures and misadventures. The sheriff swore wearily.

"What won't that hellion figure out!" he growled. "Wide-looping sheep by water!"

"It's been done before, cows too," Slade replied. "Just luck that I happened to catch on."

"I've got another word for it," said Calder. "I think those woolies must belong to Miguel Allende, from where you spotted them. He owns quite a few flocks. A Mexican-Texan and a good *hombre*. Yes, I'll ride over there some time today and let him know what happened and pick up the carcasses. Looks like you saved him something of a loss. A couple of hundred sheep runs into money. Well, you 'pear quite chipper despite your night of hell raising. Suppose we ride over to Amado's place for a bite to eat? Your gal will very likely be having the jitters."

Slade was plenty hungry himself and offered no objection to the suggestion.

"Shadow needs to put on the nosebag, too," he said. "All he's had since morning was a mesquite pod or two. I've a notion he prefers to eat over there. The stable keeper spoils him for fair. He'll be getting fat as a butterball."

"Not with the way you keep running his legs down to stumps," grunted the sheriff. "I'll get my cayuse and we'll go; won't take me but a minute."

Dolores did have a fair case of the jitters developing when they reached *La Luz*. She heaved a sigh of relief when she saw Slade, appparently still all in one piece.

"But he'll be the death of me yet, "she declared to Calder. "I never know a minute's peace anymore."

"I understand," sighed the sheriff. "You and me are in the same corral. He keeps me skittering around like a mouse on a hot skillet. And at my age! Maybe we'd be better off without him."

"Oh, he's nice to have around, at times," she smiled.

The sheriff's eyes twinkled, but he refrained from voicing an obvious comment. Dolores blushed and hurried to the kitchen to make sure their food was properly prepared.

THIRTEEN

ESTEVAN BROUGHT SLADE DISTURBING NEWS. "Something happens, *Cápitan*," he said. "Something secret. It I do not understand. Young men from the villages, the *haciendas,* they vanish. Sometimes they do not return for several days. When they reappear they are tight-lipped and explain not the reason for their absence. Tight-lipped but filled with excitement. They talk together in groups, in low tones, and desist when one walks by. What is it I do not know, but I like it not. I fear trouble comes to the River country."

Slade conferred with Sheriff Calder. "Just as I expected," he told the peace officer. "Sosna is at work, under cover. He is organizing, gathering recruits. Unless he's stopped he may kick up a real ruckus."

The sheriff tugged his mustache and swore. "Any notion what to do about it?" he asked. "We can hardly invade Mexico to run him down."

"I have an idea," Slade replied thoughtfully. "It's sort of hazy as yet and I'm not quite ready to talk about it; we'll see. By the way, did you learn anything about that steamer?"

Calder chuckled. "I did a little probing and prying," he said. "She stopped for an hour at Port Isabel, reported no cargo and skalleyhooted for the Gulf under forced draft. I've a notion she won't stop till she reaches South America. Evidently got the scare of her ornery life. Must have figured that Jim McNelty and his whole company were after them."

"That sort is seldom noted for courage," Slade remarked. "Cunning and tricky, but not looking for serious trouble. Sosna evidently got into communication with her somehow —he seems to have connections everywhere—and made a deal in which her skipper could see a profit. Didn't work out according to schedule."

"Thanks to you," said the sheriff. "Yes, those sheep belonged to Miguel Allende. He rounded them up and drove them back to pasture. I packed in the carcasses of those two devils you did for; coroner has them in his office. Hold an inquest tomorrow. Jury will set on the bodies of the

85

pastors in absentee. Allende had already packed them to his ranchhouse and prepared them for burial. He sent thanks to you. Wanted to send something else, but I knew you wouldn't accept it. He's a right *hombre*. Wonder where those hellions went to when they hightailed."

"Hard to tell," Slade replied. "Quite likely there is another ford farther west than they know of; they seem to know everything. Anyhow, I didn't think it advisable to follow him through the brush. Those poor shepherds! Sosna never leaves witnesses if he can help it."

"He left one," the sheriff returned grimly. "In which I figure he made a prime mistake."

"I hope so," Slade said. *"He's* the 'witness' that's got to be taken care of."

"He will be," Calder predicted cheerfully. "No doubt in my mind as to that. Well, let's go eat. All this palaver makes me hungry. Amado's place, I suppose? Anyhow, you'll want to be riding back with the gal later; she's okay."

Slade nodded agreement. "And there's always the chance of learning something of interest over there," he observed. "Estevan is circulating like hot water and if somebody lets something slip he'll learn of it pronto."

They found *La Luz* crowded, as usual, and it seemed to Slade that an air of repressed excitement pervaded the cantina. Matamoros, sensitive to indeterminable trouble, through bitter experience, knew something untoward was in the wind and was bracing against it.

Slade and the sheriff occupied a table and gave their orders to a waiter. Dolores came from the back room, where she was working, and sat with them for a while.

"Are you off again tonight?" she asked Slade.

"I am not," he replied. "I'm going to stay right here and take it easy."

He didn't!

They had a leisurely dinner, then smoked and talked over final cups of steaming coffee. Dolores returned to the back room and the books she was working on. After a while the sheriff joined Amado in conversation at the far end of the bar. Slade remained at the table, smoking and thinking.

It lacked an hour of midnight when Estevan came in. He strolled leisurely to Slade's table, but when he was within speaking distance his voice was urgent.

"Come at once, *Cápitan*," he whispered. "There is that

which you should see. Slowly until we are outside, then with speed."

Slade got up and they sauntered out. Once outside, however, Estevan quickened his gait to almost a run. He led the way straight to the stable.

"Saddle quickly," he said. "I think we have time, but there is none to waste. We can talk as we ride."

He was throwing a rig on a big rawboned dun as he spoke. Slade asked no questions and cinched his saddle into place with smooth speed. He was ready to ride even before Estevan was.

"First the Camino Trail," said the *vaquero*. A few minutes later they had left the town behind and were riding swiftly westward.

"Now," Slade said, "do you mind telling me what this is all about?"

"*Cápitan,*" replied the *vaquero*, "men gather. Many men. Young men. They bear rifles, and at the mid hour of the night they ride!"

"Where?"

"That, *Cápitan*, I do not know. But I thought we might follow and learn."

"You have an idea there," Slade conceded. "How many men, do you know?"

"A hundred and more," Estevan answered. Slade whistled. Looked serious.

"How did you learn this?" he asked.

"I have *amigos* who watch," Estevan said. "One learned of the gathering, one who is not stupid and who knows right from wrong. He brought me the word."

"And you don't know where they're riding? Do you know why?"

"They ride to meet with *El Libertador*.

"*El Libertador!*" he repeated, his voice hissing, scornful. "A ruthless bandit who knows no mercy. That is the *libertador* those misguided ones would follow. Follow to blood and tears and exile. *Sí*, it is the man Sosna, your enemy. He promises much. He will fulfill nothing. *Cápitan*, he must be stopped."

"Yes," Slade agreed quietly, "he must be stopped. Where is the gathering?"

"Near the village to the south and west," Estevan replied. "It is an hour's ride if we ride as we do now."

"I've a notion it wouldn't be a bad idea to speed up a little, if your horse can take it," Slade said.

"He is a good *caballo,* not the equal of yours, of course, but he will not falter," Estevan answered. He spoke to the big dun and the rawboned horse quickened his gait, Shadow smoothly keeping pace with him.

A couple of miles farther on Estevan turned from the trail and across the prairie, south by slightly west.

"It is the cut that is short," he explained. "With no mishap we will arrive in time."

The night was dark, for there was no moon and a thin mist of cloud veiled the stars which nevertheless gave enough light to make large objects discernible.

The miles flowed back under the speeding hoofs. Estevan constantly peered ahead, muttering under his breath. Suddenly he uttered an exclamation, "Ha! the village—to the right. It is distant."

Slade nodded. He had already seen the huddle of adobes, shadowy and unreal in the faint starlight.

"And now?" he prompted.

"And now, *Cápitan,* watch closely ahead and to the left," Estevan replied. "As all know, the eyes of El Halcón are as the eyes of the mountain hawk. He will see the gathering before we are seen. On a pasture near a grove; we have a mile to do."

However, Slade's unusual eyesight was not needed in this particular instance. They had covered perhaps half the distance Estevan estimated when they became aware of a glow ahead. A little farther and it materialized into the fitful flicker of a small fire. By its light Slade could make out a number of mounted figures clustered near the flames.

"They fear not detection," said Estevan. "None come here at night. Soon they will ride. Ha! they do so even now."

Evidently at a word of command, the group swung their horses around and rode almost due west across the prairie. Slade waited until they were but a moving shadow in the distance, then turned Shadow to diagonal into the direction they took. He felt confident that he and Estevan could remain unseen while keeping the large group in sight.

"See you them still, *Cápitan?*" Estevan anxiously asked a moment later. Slade nodded, still holding Shadow back.

"Madre de Dios!" marveled the *vaquero.* "I nothing can see! And my eyes are *Indio's* eyes."

"Chances are you haven't had as much experience at

looking for things in the dark," Slade replied. "Okay, speed up just a little.

"This does it," he added a few minutes later. "Now we'll amble along as we are; I can still make them out as moving shadows. Looks like they're heading for the hills."

"*Si*," replied Estevan. "*Muy malo hombres* there."

Slade was willing to agree that where the troop appeared to be heading for, very bad men were to be found.

Now the hills were looming darkly against the star strewn sky, grim, austere, desolate. The fringe of the great Sierra Madre range. Outlaw land, sanctuary for men as wild and rugged as their stony battlements and their crags.

Closer and closer drew the gaunt uprisings. And Slade could still see the drifting shadow that was the troop.

"We're following a trail, now," he said suddenly. "Not much of a one, but a trail. See, there are no glints of grassheads in the starlight, straight ahead, but there are on either side. And the hoofbeats don't sound just the same."

"I suppose *El Cápitan* is right," Estevan replied wearily. "Me, I see nothing but darkness."

Slade chuckled. "I suppose it comes up from the south and turns here," he said. "They knew where to look for it and we are following in line, so we turned into it, too."

A moment later he added, "There's a canyon mouth straight ahead; not very wide. That's evidently what they are headed for."

As they drew nearer the canyon, Slade studied the hill formations on either side, impressing them deep on the tablets of his memory.

"They're in it," he said. "I can't see them any longer. Speed up a bit, I think we can risk drawing a little closer."

Five minutes later and the canyon mouth yawned directly in their path. It was narrow and brush grown, the chaparral thinning close to the walls, especially the one to the south, near which the faint track they followed evidently ran. The ground was soft and the horses' irons made only a whisper of sound.

Slade strained his ears as they rounded a bend. "We're getting close," he breathed. "I can hear them talking. Ease up."

At that instant, only a short distance ahead, sounded, loud in the stillness, the whicker of a horse. Estevan made a frantic grab for his mount's nose. Too late! The dun answered with a shrill neigh. From ahead came a storm of alarmed exclamations. Slade whirled Shadow to the left.

"Into the brush, make for the canyon wall, quick!" he snapped.

Into the chaparral crashed the two horses. From up the trail came yells, then a bellow of gunfire. Bullets stormed down the trail, clipped leaves and twigs.

"Those *muchachos* have the trigger finger that is nervous," breathed Estevan. "Now—"

"Down the canyon," Slade interrupted. "Around the bend, then make for the trail. We're on a spot. We can't shoot at those poor misguided devils. And they're coming this way. Ride!"

They rode, with rifle reports speeding them on their way, rounded the bend and slanted toward the trail. Slade breathed relief as they reached it. He had little doubt but they would quickly out-distance the pursuit, which would probably cease at the canyon mouth. He sent Shadow forward at a fast clip, the laboring dun managing to keep up.

The trail curved through the thick brush and directly ahead was the canyon mouth. They charged from it, and practically on top of half a dozen horsemen who were coming from the opposite direction. A chorus of startled curses in good English arose. Slade saw the gleam of shifted metal, jerked both guns and fired as fast as he could pull trigger. One of the riders flopped from the saddle, a second gave a howl of pain and slumped forward in his hull. A bullet stung Slade's ribs, another ripped the sleeve of his shirt. He heard Estevan swear viciously and knew he had been nicked.

There was no chance to turn aside. They hit the group head on. Shadow met a horse shoulder to shoulder and knocked it off its feet. Which added to the wild confusion. Slade flailed right and left with the barrels of his Colts, heard one crunch on bone.

Then they were through and speeding across the prairie. Bullets whined past, but none came close. Another moment and they were out of sixgun range of the cursing, demoralized group. Bending low in their saddles they raced on against the possibility that somebody would get a rifle into action.

"You all right?" Slade asked, anxiously.

"Just the scratch," Estevan replied. "And you, *Cápitan?*"

"I'll have a couple of sore ribs, nothing more," Slade said.

90

"I hope your wild *muchachos* up the canyon keep on shooting. They might take care of a few more. I think we downed a couple, maybe. Those were some of Sosna's men headed for a rendezvous with the bunch somewhere up that infernal crack in the hills. Was sort of lively for a time and a mite hard on the nerves; we might well have been caught in a deadly crossfire."

"Of that I did not think, but it is true," answered Estevan. "It would seem, *Cápitan,* that we accomplished little."

"Perhaps more than you think," Slade differed. In fact, he felt that they had. He had carefully noted certain peculiarities of the hills for landmarks as they drew near the canyon and knew, with his instinct for distance and direction, that he could locate it again, even on the darkest night. And he felt that somewhere in the brush-grown gorge might be the answer to the problem that confronted him.

Which, however, he did not tell Estevan. The loyal *vaquero* had been exposed to enough risks; the venture he had in mind he would undertake by himself.

"Well, I think we're in the clear," he said. "Let's have a look at your arm."

"It is nothing," Estevan protested.

"Never mind, let's have a look at it," Slade repeated. "You've been losing blood."

With the aid of matches he examined the wound, which proved to be slight, and applied a pad and a bandage. He smeared a little ointment on his own grained ribs and decided that would hold him.

They reached the Camino Trail and rode on, reaching Matamoros shortly before dawn. *La Luz* was closed for business, but lights burned in the building. There they found Dolores, Sheriff Calder and Amado keeping vigil against their return. Both got a good scolding from all concerned, which did not seem to impress them much.

"See?" said Dolores. "Utterly undependable. He said he was going to stay here tonight and behave himself. And off he goes, on some wild adventure, I guarantee."

"I expect he has a good excuse," replied the sheriff. "All right, Walt, let's have it."

Slade told them, dispassionately but in detail. Dolores' breath caught in her throat. Calder muttered profanity. Amado looked decidedly worried.

91

"It would appear the *ladrone* plans a raid of some sort," he observed. "Matamoros, do you think?"

"I doubt it," Slade replied. "Not yet, at least; he'll pick an easier target first, in my opinion. If he is successful with one or two, however, Matamoros will very likely catch it, sooner or later."

"Shall we notify the *rurales*?" Amado asked. Slade shook his head.

"Not yet," he answered. "I wish to try and handle the matter with as little bloodshed as possible. Those young fellows, and, very likely, more of the same sort, are dupes. Pawns to be sacrificed in whatever game Sosna sees fit to play. Call in the *rurales* and there's a good chance that a pitched battle may result. Sosna is the key to the situation. With him disposed of, the whole thing will quickly fall apart. Also it may be possible to show the others the error of their ways. So let me see what I can do first."

"Makes sense," said the sheriff. Amado nodded agreement.

"And now," Slade said, "I think it would be a good notion for all of us to call it a night. Ready to ride, Dolores? Be seeing you, Estevan, and *gracias* for everything. Good night, Amado."

Everything considered, Slade felt that the night had been productive of results. He was positive that Sosna had not been with the bunch they met in the canyon mouth. And he thought it highly unlikely that, in the darkness and confusion, he had been recognized. There was a good chance that the outlaws would conclude that they had blundered into a couple of wandering cowhands, or a pair of owlhoots like themselves, who would be quick on the trigger, especially at night. There were plenty of masterless men in the hills. At least he hoped that would be the conclusion drawn. And he was convinced that the canyon would lead to Sosna's base of operations somewhere in the hills. If he could locate it, and stay alive in the process, he might be able to rid the section of the pest, once and for all. Surely the Sosna luck must run out sometime. That is, if it could be called luck, of which he was frankly dubious. Sheer ability was doubtless the better word.

"Well, we're up with the birdies," Dolores remarked as

they rode across the bridge. "They're already beginning to sing."

"And this particular downy bird is getting sleepy," Slade replied. "And I've got another inquest to attend in the afternoon, incidentally."

"Your big business in life, it would appear," Dolores said, with a sigh. "Well, looks like it's going to be a nice day, and Teresa will still be asleep when we get home."

"Thoughtful of her," Slade smiled.

FOURTEEN

THE INQUEST WAS HELD, the verdict similar to the last one. The sheriff was advised to get busy and run down the others responsible for the slaying of the two shepherds, who met their death at the hands of parties unknown. Back in the office, Calder remarked, "As the oldtime sailors used to say about a ghost ship, 'Ballast o' bones! ballast o' bones!' If some smart jigger would set up in the fertilizer business and just follow you around, he'd get rich. What you thinking about, Walt? You look sorta serious."

"I was wondering," Slade answered, "just where Sosna is likely to cut loose next. Unless all signs fail, he really is planning to raise some kind of a ruckus south of the Rio Grande. To do so he'll need money, plenty of it, so it's reasonable to assume that he'll be on the lookout for an opportunity to replenish his exchequer. If we could just figure what he has in mind, it would be greatly to our advantage."

"Maybe we could set a trap for the horned toad," observed the sheriff. Slade nodded.

"But it would have to be something original and out of the ordinary," he warned. "None of the time-worn expedients used to lure the garden variety of brush popping owlhoot. Sosna would see through that at once, and the trapper might well find himself the trapped. He doesn't like for anyone to underestimate his intelligence and try to make a fool of him, and shows his displeasure in no uncertain terms."

"That I can believe," nodded Calder.

Slade rolled a cigarette and for some time sat smoking in silence. The sheriff watched him but said nothing. He could see that El Halcón was doing some intensive thinking and felt it best not to interrupt.

Abruptly pinching out the butt of his cigarette, Slade stood up.

"I'm going to take a little ride," he announced. "Be seeing you."

Sheriff Calder followed his tall form out the door with

94

his eyes. He shook his head and turned back to the work on his desk.

Arriving at Jackson Street, Slade did not pause at the house but turned the corner and headed for the stable. He got the rig on Shadow and rode across the bridge to Matamoros.

Again he did not pause but rode through the town and west on the Camino Trail. He passed the ford, estimated the distance he and Estevan had covered in the course of their ride the night before, and left the trail at approximately where they had turned south. He rode south by west, veering a little less to the west than formerly. After a while he spotted a smoke smudge against the sky and knew it must rise from the village near which the young men had gathered. He did not approach the village but kept on riding south, then west, gazing toward the hills that rose against the sky.

Purposely he kept far out on the prairie, taking no chances. With Shadow between his thighs he had little fear of being cornered by an unexpected attack, but it was best to be prepared against just such an eventuality.

As he rode he studied the contours of the hills and finally arrived at the conclusion that probably the canyon could be entered other than by its east mouth. Which was important. For it was not beyond the realm of possibility that Sosna had correctly interpreted the happening of the night before, and would have the mouth of the canyon guarded. So he did not draw near the canyon but contented himself with surveying the inhospitable terrain from a safe distance. After a while he turned Shadow and rode back east by north to the Camino Trail and thence to Matamoros.

"Well, feller, I think we've sort of got the lowdown on that upended section down there," he told the horse. "So when we figure the time is ripe, we'll do a little exploring and perhaps hit on something that will bring results."

Shadow refused to commit himself pro or con. He had no intention of sticking his neck out by giving what might be bad advice for which he'd have to shoulder the blame. Slade tweaked his ear, chuckled and rode on. They were both feeling the need of the nosebag. Shadow settled for oats in his comfortable stall. Slade repaired to *La Luz* and gave his order to a waiter. Dolores sat with him while he ate and then returned to her work in the back room.

"I'll be on the floor a little later," she said. "Feel the need of some exercise. Going to dance with me?"

"How could I say no?" he replied. "Been looking forward to it all day."

"Sounds nice, anyhow," she conceded. "All right, I'll see you later, if Estevan doesn't spirit you off somewhere. That cousin of mine is getting to be a pest."

"He's okay," Slade smiled. "He takes good care of me."

"Well, don't I?"

"Have you heard any complaints?"

"Not so far," she returned laughingly, over her shoulder.

Amado came over and took the chair she vacated; he looked decidedly worried.

"There is unrest," he said. "Unrest, and whisperings. Among the *vaqueros* who tend the herds, among the *peones* of the *haciendas,* especially the younger. Unrest, and an air of expectancy. My people are mercurial, and they are superstitious. They still look to the return of their Hiawatha in his silver-white canoe. They no longer hope for a miraculous intervention from the heavens, but they do believe that sooner or later *El Libertador* will come."

"In that they are right," Slade replied gravely. "When the time is right he will come. Meanwhile the shrewd and ruthless seek to exploit their simple belief, as they have done before."

"So I fear," said Amado. "So I greatly fear." He sighed deeply and departed to attend to his chores.

A little later Estevan sauntered in to join Slade. His lips spread in the thin grin he used for a smile.

"*Cápitan*, there is great excitement," he chuckled. "The story of last night's happening has spread abroad, and it has lost nothing in the telling. Now instead of two *caballeros* riding out of the night there were a score riding the wings of the winds and casting thunderbolts from Heaven."

"A slight exaggeration, I fear," Slade smiled.

"*Sí*, but the more ignorant believe it. Some even vow they will ride no more. Against men they are willing to fight and die, but not against demons from the Pit who slay the soul as well as the body."

"Well, if that's so, we did accomplish something," Slade said. "If only a few abandon the project it may tend to shake the confidence of the others, if only a little. Another good jolt or two and the whole thing will fall apart."

"Ha!" exclaimed Estevan. "But how the jolt to give?"

"That," Slade answered, "I'll have to think on."

He was thinking on it, very seriously, and the focus of his thoughts was Veck Sosna. If he could drop a loop on that slippery gent, nothing else would be required. But, as Estevan said, how?

Sheriff Calder had suggested setting a trap for the wily outlaw. Very good, but what to bait it with? And setting a trap for Veck Sosna was like setting a snare for a sunbeam or striving to grasp a handful of morning mist.

Slightly poetic, perhaps, but nevertheless true.

Estevan glanced at the clock. "I go to meet my *amigo*," he said. "Perhaps he has learned more. Later I see you, *Cápitan?*"

"I'll be here later," Slade promised. He voiced a warning.

"Keep your eyes open, and your ears. You have been seen in my company a good deal of late. Somebody might put two and two together and make about six."

"Fear not, *Cápitan*," the *vaquero* promised. "I will have the care."

He strolled out, his keen eyes shooting glances to right and left. Slade felt he was pretty well able to take care of himself.

After a couple of dances with Dolores, Slade began to feel restless. He left the cantina and wandered about the busy streets. Matamoros slept only when it was absolutely necessary, or so it seemed. Of course the noonday *siesta* was religiously observed and folks were refreshed and wide awake in the early hours of the night.

The *Plaza de Hidalgo* was teeming. Shops and bazaars were brightly lighted. Peddlers hawked their wares. Strolling troubadours strummed guitars and sang on the corners, always with an appreciative throng around them. Sloe-eyed *señoritas* tripped along primly and had glances for the tall Ranger, who flashed his white smile in answer but kept on walking. An old *peon* leaning against a wall suddenly swept the ground with his sombrero.

"It is El Halcón!" he exclaimed. "El Halcón, the just, the compassionate. *Vaya usted con Dios!*"

"*Gracias, padre*," Slade acknowledged the greeting and slipped him a handful of small coins.

He paused for a moment near the *Casa Mata*, where there were numerous executions during the various revolutions. Openings for rifle barrels pierced the second-story walls and a large dome, probably used as a lookout post, rose

97

above the flat roof. He reflected grimly that if something wasn't soon done to remedy conditions, the sinister building might again be put in use.

Gradually he worked his way to the river and followed its curve toward the more unsavory section of the town and after a while found himself on Rio Street, where the cantina in which he and Estevan had the ruckus with the two Sosna followers was located. He had a notion that Estevan might be somewhere in the neighborhood, meeting with his *amigo* who brought him news. Perhaps he'd meet up with the *vaquero*. They'd walk back to *La Luz* together.

He paused again for a moment to gaze across the star glinted river to where the lights of Brownsville glowed golden through a thin mist rising from the water, then resumed his slow stroll.

As was habitual with him in such a section, Slade hugged the building walls, keeping in the deep shadow, his pantherlike tread practically soundless.

Ahead, less than a score of yards distant, glowed the dim light of the cantina. And about half way to the saloon yawned the mouth of a dark alley.

A man came out of the cantina, turned east, walking hurriedly. A moment more and Slade recognized Estevan. He quickened his pace, almost reached the alley and was about to raise his voice in greeting. Estevan arrived at the alley mouth first.

From the black opening darted three men who hurled themselves on the *vaquero*. Estevan, caught unprepared, nevertheless fought back viciously. It was a whirling, slugging, kicking volcano burst of activity.

Slade bounded forward, drawing his gun. He saw the flash of a knife as it flung up over Estevan's back, lashed out with all his strength. The long steel barrel of the Colt connected solidly and the knife wielder went down. A second man writhed about, hand streaking to a holster. The Colt jabbed straight out with El Halcón's sinewy arm behind it, caught the fellow squarely in the mouth. There was a crackle of splintered teeth and a howl of pain. Estevan gave him a clout on the side of the head that sent him to the ground. Slade hit the third drygulcher a glancing blow. He reeled, staggered and took to his heels, fleeing wildly west along the street.

In the alley mouth a gun blazed as Slade bounded in pursuit. The bullet fanned the Ranger's face. He whirled in

98

mid stride and, weaving and ducking, fired again and again at the flash. A screeching curse echoed the reports, and a patter of running feet.

Slade emptied his gun in the direction of the sound, jammed it into its holster and drew his lefthand Colt. Estevan, slightly dazed by the blows he had taken, was glaring about wildly and waving a cocked gun.

"Come on, let's get out of here," Slade told him. "May be more of the devils up that crack." He led the way east at a fast pace, Estevan mumbling and cursing behind him. They turned a couple of corners and neared the better lighted portion of the town. Slade slowed down to a walk. Estevan, panting for breath, drew abreast of him.

"Are you hurt?" Slade asked.

"No," the *vaquero* gulped in reply. "Just the bruises and the lumps."

"You're lucky," Slade said. "I thought I told you to be careful."

"*Cápitan,* I did have the care," Estevan protested. "All seemed well."

"Everything wasn't well," Slade replied. "And it was just by chance that I took a notion to walk this way. You're a marked man and don't your forget it. They'll be on the lookout for you again. Don't come down here again at night, and watch your step even in the daytime. Don't forget, I said."

"I will not forget," the *vaquero* promised. "*Cápitan,* my life I owe to you."

Slade knew he did but all he said was, "Be more watchful in the future. You might not get a break next time.

"Seems every time we are around that rumhole we end up in a footrace," he added. "Did you learn anything while you were there?"

Estevan shook his head. "My *amigo* he did not appear."

"And he'd better watch *his* step," Slade warned. "If they catch on to him, his life won't be worth a plugged peso. Hold it a minute under this light."

By the aid of the street lamp he examined the *vaquero's* injuries, which proved to be trifling. His face was bruised and there was a slight cut on his left hand. Thanks to his activity and Slade's timely intervention, the drygulchers haen't been able to get their knives into him. Evidently they preferred to work without noise and shot only as a last resort. Which didn't do them any good, either, and from the way one of them yelped Slade felt that one of his slugs found a mark. And a couple more were not feeling any too chipper at the moment, of that he was confident.

So, in a way, good came from evil. Without any serious mishap to Estevan, they were warned that he was included in the Sosna vendetta and would be wary in the future.

"Think you there were more of the *ladrones* in that alley?" Estevan asked.

"I don't know, but I thought it best not to take chances," Slade replied. "There could have been."

"*Sí*," agreed Estevan, "it would seem they swarm. Ha, here is *La Luz*, and I thirst. The glass of wine will be welcome."

They entered the cantina without attracting attention. Estevan ordered wine. Slade preferred coffee.

Dolores came over to the table and gave them a searching glance. Without comment she returned to the back room and secured a pad and court plaster, with which she covered the cut on Estevan's hand.

"So you got together, and evidently into trouble," she remarked.

"I did," confessed Estevan. "But *El Cápitan*, the brave, the able, he rescued me."

Followed a graphic account of the incident, stressing the part Slade played.

"You're both impossible," she declared, when Estevan paused for breath. "I hope you'll condescend to remain here the rest of the night."

"I will," Slade promised.

"And shortly I to bed go," said Estevan. "Already it is late, and with the dawn I work."

He tossed off his drink and departed. Dolores returned to her work. Slade was left to ponder the significance of the attack on Estevan and try to draw conclusions from the incident.

Of two things he was fairly certain. A closer watch was being kept on his movements than he had anticipated. His association with Estevan had been observed and a move made to eliminate the *vaquero* from his sphere of influence.

Secondly that Veck Sosna was getting a bit jumpy, appreciating the threat posed by El Halcón to his plans for fomenting an uprising among the more ignorant and susceptible of the *vaqueros* and *peones*.

Which, although he knew it exposed him to grave personal danger, Slade considered all to the good. Sosna might become reckless and as a result, more vulnerable.

The crowd was thinning out. Dolores finished her work and joined Slade.

"Shall we go?" she suggested. "There's really no reason for me to stay longer."

They rode home under the stars with very little talk, for the beauty of the night charmed them to silence.

"Would be wonderful if life could always be like this," she sighed.

"But might it not grow monotonous? Perhaps one could become surfeited with even beauty and peace."

"I think," she replied, "that that is a masculine viewpoint. I suppose a man must have a certain amount of excitement and turmoil in his life to keep him happy."

"Women, in one way or another, provide plenty of both," he chuckled.

Dolores made a face at him and gave up the argument. Biding her time for a better opportunity, when the advantage would be with her.

FIFTEEN

WHEN SLADE AROSE, EARLY IN THE AFTERNOON, he had made up his mind to a course of action.

"I doubt if I'll see you tonight," he told Dolores, as they ate breakfast together.

"Off on another wild adventure, I suppose," she predicted resignedly.

"But this won't be attended by danger," he replied. "Just a little trip of exploration."

"I don't think you could go around the corner without getting into something," she said. "You have a perfect genius for it. Sheriff Perkins was right."

"How's that?" he asked.

"He said trouble just naturally follows you around."

Slade shook with laughter. "I fear John is a pessimist," he said.

"No, he's just a realist," Dolores retorted.

"And a realist is one who interprets the facts in accordance with his own evaluation of them," he smiled.

Dolores shook her head. "You're too clever for me with your casuistic reasonings," she returned. "Anyhow, please be careful."

"I will," he promised.

Slade did not leave Brownsville until well after dark. He rode through Matamoros and west on the Camino Trail. Why was the darn thing called that, he wondered. *Camino* meant road, so the translation would be "Road Trail," which didn't seem to make sense. But that was what the people of Matamoros called it, *El Camino*, the road.

At the first bend, he drew rein and for several minutes sat gazing back the way he had come. Satisfied that he was not wearing a tail, he rode on. After a while he turned south by west across the prairie.

It was a dark night but the sky was brilliant with stars that cast a wan glow, from which groves and thickets stood out in ghostly relief. Only the occasional cry of a night bird or the yipping of a coyote broke the silence in which the patter of Shadow's irons on the grass sounded unnaturally loud.

Slade constantly studied his surroundings but nowhere appeared any cause for alarm; he was alone in a vast desolation that seemed to swing between two eternities.

Several miles north of the canyon where he had the brush with the outlaws, he turned due west and rode steadily until he reached the beginning of the hill slopes. Then he turned south and rode slowly along their base. After a while he uttered an exclamation of satisfaction.

"Here's what we're looking for, horse," he said. "See that dry wash coming down from the hills. Very little brush there, and the going shouldn't be bad. And the chances are we'll find a bit of water up toward the top, which we can use."

With which he steered Shadow into the wash that, as he predicted, was not hard to negotiate, the slope being fairly gentle and with only a scattering of undergrowth. The sides of the wash were thickly grown with flowering weeds and some grass.

A half hour of slow going and he reached the spot that was suitable for making a camp. There was a trickle of water, and sufficient grass to keep Shadow going. He removed the rig and turned the horse loose. Then he spread his blanket on a soft spot, stretched out and slept soundly till dawn.

There were staple provisions in his saddle pouches. So he kindled a small fire of dry wood and soon had bacon and eggs sizzling in a small skillet, coffee bubbling in a little flat bucket. Which, with a hunch of bread, made his simple breakfast. After washing and storing the utensils, he rolled a cigarette, sat with his back comfortably against the side of the wash and communed with Shadow.

"What we figure to do is find a way into that blasted canyon. Where we bulged into it the other night, the sides looked straight-up-and-down, but I've a notion that farther to the west they change to slopes. Maybe we can hit on one down which you can amble. I think there's a good chance that we will."

Slade paused to roll and light another cigarette; Shadow pricked his ears and looked attentive.

"When we get to the bottom," Slade resumed, "perhaps we can learn where those gents were headed for the other night, and why. I don't think there'll be anybody moseying around down there in the daytime. If I'm wrong, well, we may have the monotony broken."

Shadow snorted, as much as to say that he could do without such breaks. Slade chuckled and glanced at the brightening sky. A few minutes later he pinched out the butt, got the rig on and rode slowly up the wash. It ended on a flat bench with a rocky slope rising above.

"Looks like it's made to order for us," he told the horse. "Might reach clear to the canyon wall, which will make the going easier for you. Not much chaparral along here. Enough to fairly well hide us from anybody who might be snooping around below."

The bench petered out before it reached the canyon wall, but Slade estimated that the gorge was not more than half a mile to the south. Here he was forced to climb a long slope that led to the crest of a ridge with a wide hollow to the west. He turned south on the crest and half an hour later reached the lip of the canyon. The wall, which towered fully five hundred feet from the gorge floor, was absolutely sheer.

"Not here," he told Shadow and sent the black down the opposite sag. Crossing the bottom of the hollow he climbed the far slope to find still another depression ahead. This was also negotiated and there followed a jumble of slopes and rises which posed Shadow no great difficulty. They had covered six or seven miles of westward going when the cliffs gave place to a long slope. So far, however, it was too steep for a horse. Slade continued on his way for a few more miles.

All things come to an end, however, and finally he pulled to a halt and gazed down the brush-grown sag.

"Well, you should be able to do it here, you old goat," he said. "You've skittered down worse in your time. Let's go."

The descent was really not very difficult for a horse of Shadow's agility and sure-footedness, and they made it to the canyon floor without mishap. Slade gazed around and shook his head dubiously.

At the east mouth of the gorge the ground had been comparatively soft, but here it appeared to be floored with adamant that would leave no trace of a horse's passing. He halted Shadow and considered the situation.

"Horse," he said, "we're going to play a hunch and go east. I somehow feel those riding gents of the other night never came this far west. If I'm wrong, we can always turn around and go back."

104

Which no doubt Shadow figured was all right for him, but how about the one whose legs were being worn to stumps on these blankety-blank rocks!

However, his master didn't particularly enjoy the ride, either. It was nervous going, for there was no undergrowth that would provide cover. Run into a bunch here and there'd be nothing to do but turn tail and sift sand. And for all he knew, the west end of the canyon might be boxed, although he hardly thought so. The trail that entered the east mouth had almost certainly been an old Indian track leading somewhere far west into the high mountains.

Nevertheless, he was very much on the alert, frequently raising his eyes from the ground to gaze ahead.

Not that there was much use in studying the ground here; it was still bare rock.

The miles flowed back under Shadow's hoofs and Slade began to feel that the east mouth of the gorge could not be so very far off. He rounded a bend, ahead of which rose a bristle of brush, which was encouraging. Now he should be able to learn something.

He did, and very quickly. Where the brush began, the ground was soft, and the brush thinned near the south wall. And his keen eyes at once noted the scoring made by shod horses. He pulled up with a disgusted exclamation. Undoubtedly he had already passed the destination of the night riders. Either that, or said destination was west of where he entered the gorge. He considered the situation.

There was but one thing to do: retrace his steps, or Shadow's steps, ignore the ground over which he passed and concentrate on the walls and slopes in hope of discovering some indication that possibly his quarry might have turned aside.

Soon the sheer wall was replaced by a fairly steep slope that ended, several hundred feet above, at what appeared to be a broad bench, beyond which rose craggy hills.

But nowhere was there any evidence that a large body of men had ridden up the slope.

The cliffs resumed for a space, their summits apparently on a level with the bench. They were absolutely sheer and overhung and were scored by cracks and fissures indistinct and vague in the shadow of the overhang. He paid them little attention, for they were unclimbable by even a man on foot.

For an eighth of a mile or so the wall of dark rock con-

105

tinued, then again it gave place to a slope not a very steep one, that also ended where the bench began. Examining it with eyes that missed nothing, he rode on, his interest quickening, for a couple of hundred yards ahead were scatterings of brush; the rock floor had ended and the troop could not have traversed over the immediate terrain without leaving traces of its passage. He began quartering the ground with the greatest care. Half an hour later he pulled to a halt with an exasperated exclamation.

No horses had passed that way at any recent time.

"But where in blazes did they go?" he demanded of Shadow, who didn't have the answer. Hooking one leg over the horn, he rolled and lighted a cigarette and pondered. He was positive that nobody had gone up the slope east of the line of cliffs, for the prints showing plainly on the softer ground never turned in that direction. Presumably they continued across the stretch of rocky floor that passed the cliffs and ended before reaching the brush grown terrain where he sat his horse. Which meant somewhere in the line of cliffs lay the answer to the mystery. He would go and see.

Pinching out the butt, he turned Shadow and rode back east, hugging the base of the slope, again examining every inch of it, and found nothing.

Reaching the line of cliffs, he rode with his shoulder almost brushing the rock wall, studying it with the greatest care, with barren results.

He was passing one of the fissures, rather wider than most, a good ten feet from side to side, when something on the ground caught his eye. He pulled up, swung from the saddle and retrieved the object.

It was a length of sotol stalk, one end charred and blackened. Dry sotol stalks made excellent torches. Turning it over in his fingers, he stared at the dark mouth of the fissure. Looked like somebody might have used the thing to light his way into the crack.

Striking a match, he touched it to the stalk. It caught quickly and burned with a clear flame. Holding it aloft, he entered the fissure and walked along it for a little ways. It held a uniform width, about the same distance from the floor to the roof. Walls, floor and roof were of very dark stone. He recognized it for cooled and hardened lava.

With his knowledge of geology and vulcanology, he quickly concluded that the passage had been formed, not by the action of water, but by some tremendous explosion of steam or gasses followed by an outpouring of lava. The whole region had once been highly volcanic, and such formations were not unusual.

The floor, which was quite smooth, had an upward slant. Slade got down on his hands and knees and examined its surface by the light of the torch, which was burning low. On the lava rock, softer than the granite flooring outside the bore, were faint scratches that might have well been made by the irons of horses or the hob-nailed boots some *peones* wore.

Grinding out the butt of the torch against the wall, he returned to Shadow.

"Horse," he said, "loco as it may seem, I believe we've hit it. Anyhow, we'll go see, but not in the dark."

Mounting, he rode east to where the slope replaced the cliffs, now less than a couple of hundred yards distant; he had noted strands of sotol on the slope, where very likely the partly burned torch had come from. Dismounting, he broke off a number of the dry stalks, debated his next move.

"I'm taking enough chance, crawling into that crack, without you standing out in plain sight of anybody who might happen along," he said. "So into the brush you go, where you'll be pretty well hidden, and for Pete's sake be quiet."

The chore attended to, he retraced his steps to the fissure on foot. Lighting one of the stalks, he entered. The bore was not straight but turned and twisted, the explosive forces which formed it in past ages following the path of least resistance, and always the floor sloped gently upward, and it held to a fairly uniform width.

At first the walls and sides of the tunnel were smooth and solid lava rock, but after a few hundred yards they changed to become cracked and broken and serrated. Slade examined them by the light of his torch and experienced a wave of uneasiness. To all appearances great masses of stone were held in place by a thread, ready to fall from the vibrations set up by a loud word. His lively imagination pictured what would happen if they did break loose from the parent rock. He'd look like a stepped-on frog. Also, any such fall would undoubtedly block the bore, and as to whether there was a second opening he still did not know.

Another hundred yards or so and the utter blackness began to gray, to the accompaniment of a murmuring sound he was at a loss to account for and which loudened

107

steadily as he groped his way slowly along. Perhaps, he reflected uneasily, the sound had its origin from human activities. The devil only knew what he was barging into. He slowed his pace and hugged the rock wall, rounded one of the many turns, and felt the howling gust of a wind which nearly swept him off his feet; it was the wind that was responsible for the sound, now rising to a bellow. And now he saw where the light came from, and it was a view that was appalling in its gloom and grandeur, and calculated to shake the nerve of the strongest.

SIXTEEN

THE TUNNEL HAD ENDED AT THE VERGE OF A MIGHTY CHASM in the black rock, jagged and torn and splintered throughout by some awful convulsion of nature in past ages, as though it had been cleft by stroke on stroke of lightning or the downward sweep of a fiery "sword of vengeance."

Up and up soared the cliffs that walled the chasm, with a narrow strip of sunlit sky lying on their crests, from which seeped the gray light. And along the edge of the frightful gulf ran a ledge not more than five feet wide. Above were space on space of giddy air; below, black depths of emptiness. The roaring draught that sucked down the chasm drove misty wreaths of vapor before it, blinding the eyes and confusing the senses.

For hundreds of yards the Ranger followed this path of terrors, which sloped steadily upward. He heaved a breath of thankfulness when the chasm ended and the solidly floored tunnel resumed once more. A few more hundred paces and again he saw light.

The bore ended in an almost circular amphitheatre, walled about by sheer cliffs some fifty or sixty feet in height. There was a fringe of vegetation overhanging their crests.

The depression was, of course, a former blowhole or minor crater when the region was beset by volcanic activity. Through the course of the eons since the volcano had become extinct, erosion from the cliff crests had built up the floor and at the same time reduced the height of the cliffs that had been the crater's sides.

Here was Sosna's parade ground, where he drilled his "troops" that would make up the efficient and disciplined striking force which would be something to reckon with if he ever got going strong.

Near the far wall of the crater, which was something more than a hundred yards in diameter, was a squat building that looked to be one solid block of stone, for it was walled and roofed by slabs of lava rock. Slade instantly recognized it as a former Aztec temple, unused for many years. The Aztecs, he knew, had a penchant for erecting their temples, especially those to Quetzalcoatl, the god of air, the light and the storms, in unusual places.

Which explained how Sosna had learned about the place. The memory of such things being kept alive from generation to generation.

Slade crossed the bowl and entered the temple. All about were signs of recent occupancy and use. There were tumbled blankets scattered about, rude fireplaces of stone, stores of staple provisions, and long lines of rifles standing against one wall, brand new and of modern make. Also, numerous boxes of ammunition. The outlaw leader had an ambitious project in mind.

But very quickly he concluded that this was not Sosna's hangout; all signs pointed to but temporary occupancy from time to time. Well, he had learned something. He knew now where the riders of the night he and Estevan trailed were headed for, and the inference was that they would gather here again in the near future. He left the temple and studied the cliffs that walled the amphitheatre.

With a nod of satisfacton, he bestowed a last glance around the crater. Better be getting out while the getting was good; if the bunch happened to show up, he'd be neatly trapped.

Trapped? Sheriff Calder had suggested the possibility of setting a trap for Sosna. Well, if developments of the next hours were what he hoped they'd be, here might well be opportunity to set a trap, if he could just manage to spring the darn thing without getting his own comeuppance. He threaded his way back through the cave-tunnel, pausing briefly to more thoroughly examine the cracked and broken walls and roof of the bore, then hurrying to where he left Shadow.

Mounting, he sent the big black up the slope, reaching the bench without serious difficulty. It was heavily brush grown but Shadow managed to worm his way through it with a minimum of scratches. Slade rode due west, keeping a sharp watch on the terrain ahead and letting Shadow take his time.

As he anticipated, the crater opened onto the bench. Slade dismounted, forced his way through the chaparral to its lip and gazed at the scene below. Once again he nodded with satisfaction.

"Horse," he said, "I believe it will work, but with odds

of a hundred and more against us, we've got to be careful. Okay, I've seen all I want to see, let's head for the nosebag. My stomach is thinking my throat has been sewed up, and I've a notion you're feeling a mite lank, too."

Reaching the canyon floor, he diagonaled across to the long slope that led down from the hills and rode steadily, arriving at Matamoros a couple of hours before sunset.

After seeing that Shadow was properly cared for, he entered *La Luz*, found a vacant table and ordered everything in sight.

Dolores greeted him warmly and with evident relief, as did Amado. "I declare I've held my breath ever since you left," the girl said.

"Then you should be red in the face, but you're not," Slade answered. Dolores did not pursue the conversation.

"Seen anything of Estevan?" he asked.

"He will be in later," Amado replied. "He waited for you last night, on the chance you might appear."

"I'll wait for him tonight," Slade promised.

His dinner finished, Slade relaxed with coffee and a cigarette and went over the details of the plan he had evolved. It was a daring plan, and the undertaker would be smiling over his shoulder every minute as he put it into effect; but he believed it would work. A chance that he might be able to drop a loop on Sosna, and an even better chance to frustrate the contemplated uprising. Worth the risk, he felt.

Altogether he considered the day's exploration a success. He had learned most of what he set out to learn. The whereabouts of Sosna's hangout was still a mystery, but if his plans developed as he hoped, the importance of that might well be minimized.

With a mind free from care, for the moment, he threw himself into the spirit of hilarity which characterized the cantina. He had several dances with Dolores and, at her suggestion, with a couple of the floor girls. He yielded to the request of the orchestra leader and sang for the gathering, his offerings received with great applause.

"You can be delightfully cheerful and entertaining when you take a notion to be," Dolores complimented him.

"Always entertaining, and satisfactorily so?"

Dolores blushed, and refused to commit herself.

"Your ego doesn't need any bolstering," she told him.

It was quite late when Estevan finally arrived. "I was

111

worried," he said, as he sat down and accepted a glass of wine. "I feared something bad had happened."

"Nothing to bother about," Slade replied. "I just took a little ride."

"And the ride was one of profit?"

Slade hesitated, then told him everything, for he felt he had a right to know. Estevan swore in three languages.

"And you have a plan, *Cápitan?*"

"Yes, I have a plan," Slade answered. "But I will need your help. Do you think you can learn when the young men will ride again?"

"My *amigo* will learn and will tell me," Estevan assured him. "I will meet with him tomorrow; we do not meet on Rio Street any more."

"A good notion," Slade said. "Wouldn't be surprised if that place on Rio Street is being watched."

The following afternoon, Slade visited Sheriff Calder. He handed the official a slip of paper.

"Things I want you to buy for me," he explained. "You should be able to do it without occasioning comment."

Calder stared at the list and whistled. "A half dozen sticks of dynamite, caps and a coil of fuse," he enumerated the list. "What in blazes are you going to do, blow up the town?"

"No, but I hope to blow somebody's plans sky high," Slade replied.

"You mean Sosna's?"

"Yes," Slade admitted. "That's all I think you should know for now. What I have in mind will sort of fracture International Law, but in a good cause."

"You're the limit!" Calder declared. "All right, I'll mosey out and get the stuff. I hope you don't blow yourself up."

"I'll try not to," Slade promised. Privately he thought there was a chance to do just that.

A couple of uneventful days followed, during which the Ranger chafed with impatience. He continually expected to hear that Sosna had cut loose somewhere, with very likely bloodshed and murder attendant.

All he could do, however, was while away the time and wait. He and Dolores took a long ride across the range-land to the north. He visited with Sheriff Calder and spent the evenings and nights at *La Luz,* hoping for word from Estevan, who failed to put in an appearance.

Late the second night, the *vaquero* did appear with the word.

"Tomorrow they ride," he said. "Tomorrow at the mid hour of the night. Many more than a hundred this time."

"*Gracias, amigo,* Slade replied. "You have helped me greatly."

"*Cápitan,* do you plan to ride again to that thrice accursed canyon?" Estevan asked. Slade nodded.

"Let me go with you," Estevan pleaded. Slade shook his head.

"Not this time," he said. "I can handle the chore better alone."

He had no intention of exposing the *vaquero* to the hazards of the mad venture.

Estevan looked sad but did not further urge him, knowing it would be useless.

"Tonight I burn the candles to my patron saint, that he will watch over you and give you safe return," he said.

"Thank you, Estevan," Slade answered. "Prayer never hurt any man and can guard against evil."

SEVENTEEN

SLADE TOLD NO ONE ELSE WHAT HE HAD IN MIND, not even Dolores. He could see no sense in needlessly worrying her. Either he would be all right or he wouldn't be, so why bother about what the future had in store.

Shortly after dark the following day, Slade left Matamoros. After making sure he was not followed, he rode south by west across the prairie at a fast pace. Tonight there was a sickle of moon hanging low in the west and the level land was fairly well lighted.

It was different, however, when he reached the hills. The moon had gone down and he had only the faint glimmer of the stars to guide him as he rode slowly up the rises and down the sags. But he was confident his plainsman's instinct for distance and direction would keep him on the right track. Finally he descended the long slope into the canyon and a little later found himself ensconced in the growth east of the cave mouth, from where he could see and not be seen.

A long and tedious wait followed, the monotony alleviated only by an occasional cigarette. He began to wonder if Estevan's informant had been mistaken.

Finally, however, his vigil was rewarded. To his ears came the thud of many hoofs beating the canyon floor, and the sound came from the east. He tensed to watchfulness.

The company came into view, grotesque, distorted in the gloom, devoid of detail, stealthily approaching unreality born of the darkness of the night. A shadow drifted past his hiding place and continued beyond the cave opening. There the light was a little better. He saw the riders dismount, pass in behind the growth and knee hobble their mounts, then make their way to the cave mouth, into which they quickly vanished. Slade settled himself for another wait. Better not to take chances. Others might follow the first group.

He recalled now that he had paid scant heed to the belt of growth beyond the cliffs, for his attention had been centered on the slope. Otherwise he could hardly have failed to notice that horses had been tethered there from time to time. He strained his ears to detect the possible approach of more riders.

But the night remained utterly still; nothing moved amid the brush. After nearly an hour had elasped he stole forth and approached the cave. At the mouth he paused to listen; the dark bore was silent as a tomb. He entered and walked swiftly up the slanting floor, for he knew there were no pitfalls, nothing to stumble over. Not until he heard the distant murmur of the wind soughing down the chasm did he halt and chance lighting one of the torches he carried, along with the bundle of dynamite and the percussion caps and the coil of fuse.

He stuck the torch into a crevice and, working swiftly and expertly, inserted the lethal greasy cylinders into other crevices making sure they were firmly seated. He capped and fused them, cutting the lengths of fuse with the utmost nicety. When all was finished, he listened another moment, then touched the flame of the torch to the fuse ends, watched the sparks and the spurtle of smoke appear.

Dashing out the torch, he whirled and raced down the bore at top speed. There was no telling how far the effects of the blast might extend, and there was always the danger of a premature explosion.

The tunnel abruptly seemed endless, the time he had calculated for the fire to reach the cartridges surely drawn to a close. His heart pounded, his breath came in gulps. He realized what he had hardly noticed before, how stagnant was the air of the tunnel.

He had barely reached the cave mouth and was reeling a little, when he heard the ominous roar of the exploding dynamite, which almost instantly was followed by a stupendous crashing and rumbling that continued for seconds.

A blast of displaced air howled past, almost knocking him off his feet. "Blazes!" he muttered. "Looks like it brought the whole darn thing down from one end to the other."

Leaning against the cliff for a moment to catch his breath, he experienced an exultant glow. The first part of his plan was highly successful. Sosna's "army" was neatly trapped, with only himself to depend on for deliverance from their rock-walled prison. He felt he was in an excellent bargaining position.

As for the captives, let them stew in their own juice for

115

a while, which should make them more tractable when the time for discussion arrived. Well, better get back to his hideout against the chance of somebody coming along. Mustn't play his luck too strong; so far he'd gotten the breaks.

With which he returned to where Shadow, concealed in the brush, was contentedly cropping grass. Slade scooped a couple of handfuls of oats from his saddle pouches to help hold down the herbage, which the black horse received with dignified appreciation. Slade stretched out on his blanket and drowsed, knowing that his mount would notify him of anybody approaching, which he now didn't think was likely for the time being.

When the east began to glow with dawn he roused up and munched a couple of sandwiches he had brought with him, washing them down with a canteen of cold coffee, for he did not dare light a fire and cook. Then, confident there would be no important developments in the near future, he really went to sleep for a couple of hours, awakening much refreshed.

He slipped to the edge of the growth and peered up and down the canyon. Nowhere was there any sign of life. He returned to Shadow, rolled a cigarette and smoked thoughtfully.

"After a while we'll have a little palaver with our *amigos* in durance vile," he told the horse. "By then I've a notion they'll be quite subdued and ready to be reasonable."

He decided to wait a while longer. Soon it would be time for *siesta*, which the captives wouldn't get and would be feeling a bit low in consequence.

So he lounged and smoked until the sun was past the zenith. Then he got the rig on Shadow and sent him up the slope at a leisurely pace. Reaching the bench, he rode west until he was near the crater. Dismounting he stole forward until he could peer through a final fringe into the pit. What he saw was quite satisfactory.

Some of the hundred and more men below were prowling about like caged beasts. Others slumped in attitudes of dejection. All looked depressed, haggard and generally in anything but good spirits. Slade felt the time was ripe for action.

He did not expose himself, for there might be some of Sosna's immediate followers in the milling crowd and it was best not to take chances with a nervous trigger finger.

116

His voice rang out, rolling in thunder across the pit, "*Amigos, atención!*"

A volley of startled exclamations arose. All eyes turned to the crater lip. A voice called, "Who speaks?"

"El Halcón," Slade replied. An excited murmur ran through the gathering.

"El Halcón! The just, the honorable, the friend of the lowly!"

"Yes, El Halcón," Slade said, in fluent Spanish. "Listen, friends, you have been duped and deceived. Your liberator is no true liberator, but a ruthless bandit who would sacrifice you to his own evil ends. Even now you face lingering death. I tell you, he is no true liberator."

Again the murmur, louder this time.

"If El Halcón says it is so, it *is* so. Save us, *Cápitan*."

"I will save you, on a condition," Slade answered.

"*Sí, Cápitan, sí?*"

"Yes. That you disband, return to your homes and live in peace and honor till the day of justice arrives, which is not yet. You have the word of El Halcón. Depend on your liberator to save you and you will die the horrible death of starvation. But do you prefer to trust yourselves to him rather than El Halcón, *adios*—"

A wail of anguish rose from the pit. "Nay, nay, *Cápitan*, do not leave us to perish. El Halcón we trust and believe; that *ladrone* we no longer do. Do not leave us, *Cápitan*."

"Very well," Slade replied. "Are any of the liberator's men down there with you?"

"None. Today we were to drill, with our sergeants commanding."

"When is the liberator—the *ladrone*—supposed to come here?"

"He comes at sundown, *Cápitan*, or so we were told."

Slade stepped into view. A cheer went up as his tall form appeared on the cliff crest, and shouts of "El Halcón! It is indeed El Halcón!"

Slade smiled down at them. "You have nothing more to fear. Have you water down there?"

"*Sí, Cápitan*, there is always a trickle back of the old temple.

"Then," Slade said, "eat, drink and be merry, for tomorrow you do *not* die. Tomorrow friends will come with ropes and slings to rescue you. Have yourselves a picnic, and siesta."

A roar of laughter greeted the sally, and more cheers. The mercurial Latins, their cares lifted, with nothing to worry about, chattered gaily among themselves. Some ran to kindle fires and cook. Slade waved his hand and returned to his hiding place. He made himself comfortable and schooled himself to patience.

The afternoon wore on, filled with sunlight and peace. Birds sang, little animals went about their various businesses, a faint breeze whispered musically through the leaves. Finally shadows began creeping across the canyon floor. Slade got the rig on his horse and made sure he was well concealed.

The sun sank behind the western crags and the canyon grew gloomy. And from the east sounded the thud of hoofs.

Tense, alert, Slade peered through the leafy screens. Another moment and four riders bulged around the bend. In the lead was tall, flashing-eyed Veck Sosna. Slade breathed an exasperated oath as frustration tugged at his heart.

There, within easy sixgun range, was his quarry, but he couldn't do a darn thing about it. Sosna would not surrender, and the others would follow his lead. The odds were too great. Not only would his own life be at stake but a hundred other lives. Without his help, the poor devils in the pit were doomed. Sosna would not take the trouble to rescue them, even did he know how to go about it, which Slade was confident he didn't.

Seething with impotent anger, he watched the four ride on to the cave mouth. He fingered the butts of his guns but dared not draw them. He had to contact Estevan who would pass the word to the villages and organize a rescue party. He just couldn't afford to take a chance.

The outlaws rode past the cave mouth and hobbled their horses with the others. They returned at a leisurely pace and entered the cave. Slade settled back to wait.

He didn't have very long to wait. Very shortly the four reappeared, talking excitedly. They made for their horses, loosed them and mounted. Another moment and they were riding east at a fast clip. Sosna's bell-toned voice rang out, "To hell with them! Let them starve, if they didn't get caught beneath the fall. Who cares; I can get others."

A flame of wrath enveloped El Halcón, almost blinding him with its intensity. He longed to shoot the callous devil in the back, but he could not. Even here on Mexican soil he was still bound by the code of the Rangers.

Chafing with impatience, he waited minutes. The canyon was growing quite dark. He mounted and sent Shadow drifting after the unsavory quartet. He rode vigilant and alert, although he did not expect them to draw rein in the canyon. When he reached its mouth he spotted them, a dark smudge traveling north by slightly east. Again he waited, until the moving smudge was barely discernible. He was confident that with his unusually keen eyesight he could keep it in view. He rode on hopefully; he might get a lucky break in one way or another.

Sosna and his men continued steadily. The miles flowed back under Shadow's hoofs and Slade never lost sight of the moving smudge.

Finally the Camino Trail came into view, a grayish ribbon against the background of the night. The quarry reached it, turned east, as if Matamoros was their destination.

Evidently it wasn't. At the ford, they turned north and sent their horses into the water. Slade wished he were closer; he might have taken the chance of staging a gun fight, with the odds a bit more even. He speeded up and when Sosna and his men reached the far bank he saw that they turned east. Looked very much like they were headed for Brownsville. Slade altered his course a little and slanted more to the east, reaching the Camino near the environs of the town. He rode straight to *La Luz,* dismounted and hurried in, hoping he would find Estevan present.

He wasn't. Slade beckoned Amado and the owner at once sent men to try and round up the *vaquero.* Slade stabled his horse, returned to the cantina, curbed his impatience and proceeded to fortify himself with a good dinner. He could do nothing more until he talked with Estevan. He dared not relay the information through a third party; there might be a slip somewhere and if something happened to him during the night, which was not improbable if he managed to find Sosna in Brownsville, the prisoners in the pit would suffer.

Dolores came over and sat with him. He told her everything. She listened in silence till he had finished, her eyes glowing.

"What a wonderful thing you did," she said. "Now there will be no uprising, no senseless bloodshed and loss of innocent lives. The women of the villages will remember

119

you in their prayers, and so will many here in Matamoros when the truth is known, and so will I, as always."

Slade bowed his head reverently. "And the prayers of a good woman come before a man as a shield from evil," he replied.

"But you are still pursuing that awful man?" she asked.

"Yes, I'm still pursuing him," Slade answered, adding grimly, "And I've a notion he's about reached the end of his twine."

"I hope so," she said, "because until he does, neither of us will know peace."

EIGHTEEN

AN HOUR DRAGGED PAST, WITH NO ESTEVAN. Slade was in a fever of impatience, for he felt that Sosna and his bunch were somewhere in Brownsville, with no guarantee how long they would remain there. The hellion might even be planning to pull out of the section altogether, and if so, the wearisome hunt for him would have to begin all over again.

Finally Estevan put in a tardy appearance, having been intercepted by one of Amado's couriers.

Slade related the happenings of the night and day and concluded with explicit directions as to how to locate and reach the crater rim.

"Take ropes and slings," he said. "And first see how those horses are making out; I didn't have time to look after them. Should be okay, though, they were knee-hobbled and there was water and plenty of grass within reach. Take your time and make sure everything is as it should be. The boys down in the hole are doing all right by themselves and it won't hurt them to stay there a few hours longer. Will give them a chance to reflect on the error of their ways."

Estevan's admiration was boundless. "Truly El Halcón is a magic name," he declared. "Long will it be remembered."

He hurried out to organize the rescue party. Slade got the rig on Shadow and rode across the bridge.

His first stop was the sheriff's office, where a deputy on duty there told him that Calder was at the saloon on Jefferson and Fourteenth Streets having a bite to eat.

Calder listened with interest to Slade's account of his recent adventures.

"So it looks like we won't be dodging revolution lead over here," he commented. "For which everybody will be thankful to you. And you figure Sosna might be somewhere in town? Yes? And you're going hunting for him?"

"I am, and right away," Slade replied.

"And I'm going with you," the sheriff said, decisively.

"Never mind any arg'fyin', now. I'm sheriff of this county and it's my duty to apprehend law breakers in my bailwick. Four of the devils, you say? Well, four against two is better than one against four; odds won't be so blankety-blank lopsided. And I'm itching to line sights with that hyderphobia skunk. Let's go!"

Without further delay they began their search. Slade looped the split reins into place, spoke to Shadow. The black horse ambled along beside him.

"Taking him with you, eh?" the sheriff commented.

"Trailing Veck Sosna without a horse handy is a fine way to end up holding the hot end of the branding iron," Slade replied. "He always seems to have his mount close by and once he gets in the saddle he's something to reckon with. He's a fine judge of horse flesh and always manages to tie onto a really top critter. Shadow will go wherever we go."

"Wouldn't be surprised if he ambles into a bar and snorts for a snort," Calder chuckled.

"Captain Jim insists he's got more brains than I have," Slade said with a smile.

"Well, they say a feller needs horse sense to get to the top," replied Calder. "I've a notion sometimes that's right. Anyhow, this one sure ain't terrapin-brained. Well, let's see what's in the joint."

They observed nothing of interest in the first saloon they visited and moseyed on.

"Which is the best way to go, do you figure?" Calder asked.

"I'd suggest we give Fourteenth a whirl first," Slade said. "It runs to the river and the bridge, and there are some rumholes close to the river that should appeal to Sosna's kind. No luck there and we might work over to Fronton Street, which runs along close to the *Estero*. I've noticed some prime spots there, around Fourth and Fifth Streets.

"But," he added, "Veck Sosna is like gold. The old saying goes that gold is where you find it, and that applies to Sosna. No telling where he might be if he's still in town. Well, all we can do is keep looking, and hope."

Place after place on Fourteenth Street and its environs proved barren of results. After a while they worked their way west to Fronton Street. There they visited establishments that were enough to curl a coyote's hair, and where the sheriff's entrance provoked a certain nervousness on the part of the patrons. But nowhere did they find hide or hair of the men they sought.

As a last resort they combed St. Francis and St. Charles Streets with no results. Calder swore in weary disgust.

"Looks like the hellions didn't stop in Brownsville but kept on going to maybe Port Isabel," he growled.

"Maybe, but I doubt it," Slade said. He leaned against a lamp post, rolled a cigarette and smoked thoughtfully, gazing toward the Rio Grande. Calder waited patiently for any suggestion he might make.

Carefully pinching out the butt and casting it aside, Slade turned to the sheriff.

"Tom," he said, "we're going to follow a hunch. First we'll tie onto your cayuse and then we'll ride. Incidentally, you can unpin your badge and shove it in your pocket. Where we're going the only authority we'll pack is what we've got tied to our waists; but I believe that if we start something we can get away with it."

"Matamoros, eh?" remarked Calder as they headed for the stable.

"That's right," Slade replied. "I've a notion that if the hellion stopped in Brownsville at all it was but for a short time. Then he slid across the river. If he is over there, I've an idea where he may be holed up. Just playing a hunch, but it may pay off."

"Well, nothing else has, so we might as well give it a whirl," the sheriff agreed.

Half an hour later the hoofs of their horses thudded on the floor boards of the bridge.

As they crossed the bridge, Slade noted a ship at the wharf back of *La Luz* getting up stream preparatory to departure down the river. She looked to be a sea-going tramp.

When they reached the Mexican shore, Slade circled around through the town and approached Rio Street from the west.

"As I said, I'm playing a hunch," he repeated. "I've just got a feeling that I know where the hellion is liable to be holed up—he's been there before. If we get a break, we may find him there. If we do, don't take any chances. Try and shoot first, and shoot fast and straight."

Finally they drew near the dingy cantina *El Toro*, where Slade and Estevan had the brush with the outlaws. There were hitchracks on either side of the saloon, at a little

123

distance from its door. Slade chose the one to the west, dismounted and dropped the split reins to the ground. Sheriff Calder tied his horse.

With quick light steps they approached the door, Slade slightly in front, hands close to his guns, Calder crowding beside him. Slade flung open the swinging doors and they were inside the cantina.

There wasn't a very large crowd present. Slade shot a swift glance all around, muttered his disgust.

"Not here," he told his companion.

Their entrance had occasioned only casual glances. Slade sauntered to the bar.

"Might as well have a drink," he remarked. "Well, looks like I fluffed this one. I felt positive the hellion would be here. Just a case of wishful thinking, I guess."

"Can't be right all the time," Calder replied cheerfully. "Maybe we'll find him someplace else."

"I doubt it," Slade said morosely. "Nope, we might as well admit we followed a cold trail. We'll mosey over to Amado's place, isn't so far off, and see if we can pick up any information there."

They finished their drinks, turned toward the door and took a couple of steps.

NINETEEN

THE DOORS SWUNG BACK AND FOUR MEN STARTED TO ENTER. The first three were blocky, swarthy-faced individuals. The fourth, slightly behind the others, was tall, flashing-eyed.

"Look out!" Slade roared, and went for his guns. Instantly the peace of the cantina exploded in bellowing action. Both Slade's guns cut loose with a rattling crash as flame and smoke gushed from the group in the doorway. He saw a man fall. A second went down as the sheriff's Colt boomed. A slug ripped through his hat. Another burned a red streak along his neck. He heard Calder grunt and knew he had been nicked.

A third outlaw floundered sideways and hit the floor. But, shielded by the falling body, Veck Sosna's tall form vanished from sight.

Slade bounded forward, slammed into a man frantically trying to get out of the line of fire, almost lost his balance, surged forward again and had to haul a second man out of his path. At the door he slipped and floundered over the three bodies scattered there, in his ears ringing the clatter of fast hoofs fading away. He fought his way through the door and saw Sosna, mounted on a splendid bay horse and fleeing madly eastward. He sped to where Shadow stood, flung himself into the saddle and raced in pursuit, unsheathing his rifle.

But as he clamped the weapon to his shoulder, Sosna swerved to the right and whisked around a corner, apparently bound for the water. Slade ground his teeth in exasperation and shouted to Shadow for greater speed. He had to slow a little turning the corner, and saw Sosna vanished around the next one, still heading east. A moment later and he, too, was around the corner and on the street running next to the water. Sosna had gained and was now well ahead.

"But you're not going to outrun Shadow, blast you," Slade muttered. "This looks like *it*."

Back of *La Luz*, the ship Slade had noted as they crossed the bridge was slowly pulling away from the wharf, gangplank lifted, stack puffing. He saw Sosna again swerve to the right, heard the thunder of his horse's hoofs on the

125

wharf planks. Straight for the widening strip of water the outlaw dashed, his voice rang out. The bay horse gathered himself together and jumped.

It was a mighty leap, but he soared through the air like a bird and made it, his irons thudding solidly on the steamer's deck.

From the ship rose amazed shouts that changed to yells of terror as Sosna's gun boomed, and again, and he leaped from his horse, roaring commands. They were instantly heeded by the terrified wheelsman and skipper. The stack bellowed, vomiting clouds of smoke, the ship's bow swung around, pointing straight for the middle of the river, and she plowed forward, gathering speed at every turn of her screw.

Seething with impotent fury, Slade pulled to a halt on the wharf, rifle at the ready, trying to get a glimpse of Sosna; but it was impossible to single him out among the figures swirling about the shadowy deck. He was still sitting there, the useless rifle in his hand, when the sheriff clattered up beside him.

"Did you get him?" Calder bawled. "Where'd he go?"

Slade gestured to the departing ship. "His luck still held," he replied. "There he goes, with his luck and a hairtrigger mind that instantly recognizes opportunity and takes advantage of it. The luck part was that the infernal ship had to be pulling out at just that moment."

"Well, have her intercepted at Port Isabel and grab him," Calder exclaimed excitedly.

Slade laughed mirthlessly. "Long before they reach the Point, Sosna will force them to put him ashore somewhere," he replied. "No, there's no use bothering about him any more for the present. He's made good his escape. Oh, well, maybe another time—

"You all right?" he asked. "Thought you stopped one."

"Just a scratch," Calder said. "Lost a little hunk of meat from my left arm; bleeding's about stopped already. Now what?"

"Got 'em dead center," Calder replied.

"Around the corner, stable our horses and drop in at Amado's place," Slade answered. "We don't know anything. Those three hellions done for?"

"The *alcalde* will take care of the carcasses," Slade said. "Well, at least you are rid of the pest in this section. Good luck to you, bad luck to somebody else."

"We can stand a little," grunted Calder.

Heads were peering cautiously from the back windows of the cantina, but nobody ventured out. After stabling their mounts, Slade and the sheriff entered. Amado and Dolores were anxiously awaiting them.

"Did not we hear shooting in back?" Amado asked.

"Seems they had quite a ruckus on the ship that just pulled out," Slade replied, with truth. At a table he told them just what happened.

"And the *ladrone* got away!" growled Amado.

"As usual," Slade replied. "Oh, well, all in a day's work."

"And I suppose you'll be leaving now?" Dolores said.

"Yes, I'll have to leave within a day or two," he answered. "I've been away from the Post a long time as it is. Captain Jim will have another little chore lined up for me when I get back."

Dolores sighed, her beautiful eyes wistful, but did not otherwise comment.

"I'll order you something to eat," she said.

"And you come to the back room for a moment," Amado said to the sheriff. "I'll patch up your arm."

Some little time later, while they were eating, the *alcalde* strolled in.

"Pedro's been here three times already, looking for you," Amado chuckled. "I told him of the uprising that is no more. He was much pleased."

Smiling broadly, the mayor came straight to the table and held out his hands.

"*Gracias, amigo!*" he said to Slade. "In behalf of the people of Matamoros and elsewhere, I thank you."

Slade smiled and bowed and they shook hands. The mayor beamed at him paternally.

"We could use more such excellent young men as yourself," he said. "By the way, it would seem there was trouble down on Rio Street tonight, or so I was told. Well, well, hot blood can only be cooled by letting it flow now and then. And at times thereby, justice is done."

With a smile and a bow he departed.

Slade and Dolores crossed the bridge together, and two days later, sadly but with a light of hope in her eyes, she watched him ride away, tall and graceful atop his great black horse, to where duty called and new adventure waited.

WALT SLADE

Greatest of the Texas Rangers

Follow the action-packed adventures of this undercover ace in this exciting western series.